LIGHT BLUE WITH BULGES

LIGHT BLUE WITH BULGES

Nick Sedgwick

FOURTH ESTATE · LONDON

First published in Great Britain in 1989 by
Fourth Estate Ltd
Classic House
113 Westbourne Grove
London W2 4UP

British Library Cataloguing in Publication Data
Sedgwick, Nick
  Light blue with bulges
  I. Title
  823'.914 (F)

ISBN 1-872180-05-1

Typeset in Bauer Bodoni by York House Typographic Ltd, London W7
Printed and bound in Great Britain by The Guernsey Press, Guernsey

For my real parents,
and for Carey

1

I was seventeen, I'd just left school, and I was certain I'd live for ever. Now my father was telling me I had to get a job. All of a sudden I felt old before my time. The friends I'd grown up with were going off to college; for them it was three effortless years of fornication and fun. Yet here I was, Ned Selby, undiscovered genius, about to become a drudge. Was it fair? No, the answer came back, it certainly wasn't.

'All right, my lad,' my father was saying. 'Have you thought about what you're going to do with your life?'

I hadn't. A road stretched ahead of me, a minor road winding off into the murky distance, occasionally circumventing indistinguishable obstacles. I had two O levels. I was supposed to be good at English.

'I'm supposed to be good at English,' I said brightly.

He peered at me, eyes determinedly wide behind his spectacles. They were the half-lens variety. He had an idea they did something for his appearance, made him look distinguished. When they slipped down the blade of his nose, forcing him to frown over them, they made him look ferocious but the trick had never fooled me.

'So you damn well should be,' he said curtly, his spectacles already on the move. 'It's your native language. Where's the achievement in being good at English? I'm good at English. Your mother's good at English. What else are you good at?'

He frowned, tilting his head.

I shrugged, thinking hard.

'You're a drifter,' he said. 'You're good at drifting.'

I was indignant.

'What does that mean?' I asked. 'I've lived in this house all my life. I've been to the same school all my life. How can I be a drifter?'

'You lounge. You listen to jazz.'

The last word hissed, then lingered.

'That makes me a lounger, a listener. It doesn't make me a drifter.'

'Ach,' he said disgustedly. It was a strange, gutteral sound, harsh and Germanic. 'Well, you've got six weeks. If you want to go on living in this house after that you'd better go and find a job.'

A job! I shrank from the very word. I'd had jobs ever since I was fourteen, when I'd been told I was old enough to find holiday jobs. Holiday jobs! How could this be, I'd wondered. Big jobs, bad jobs, maybe even good jobs, though I'd thought this was stretching it. But holiday jobs! Even to my callow fourteen-year-old intelligence the two ideas were

2

mutually exclusive. Still, I did as I was bid. I trudged the streets, pounding on doors.

He wasn't a bad sort, my father. But he'd come up the hard way: apprenticeship at twelve, evening classes for ten years, no time for sex or other niceties, a slow ascent up the professional ladder. Against all the odds he'd made something out of himself. It wasn't that he didn't like what he'd made, a civil servant in the Ministry of Agriculture, it was just that he knew what he might have been, how far he might have gone, if he'd had the educational opportunity he'd been denied, and was now giving me. Naturally, I was wasting it. Jobs were part of the deal. They were supposed to concentrate the mind. Two summer months of casual labour every year would be enough to serve notice on a future without O levels. I'd knuckle down, become an A student.

First I picked fruit. To this day my stomach still heaves at the smell of blackcurrants. Then I was a van boy in a brewery. Christmases, I delivered the mail. I washed floors in a sausage and meat-pie factory. The only job which came close to concentrating my mind was the one I had in the stockroom of a big department store, unpacking panties. I was sixteen. The panties weren't cheap nylon trash with cotton gussets, they were silk, the real thing, so light I could barely feel their weight, soft but crisp too. Pinks, light blues, blacks and whites. I had my favourites. All day I had a bone on just handling the stuff. I couldn't help thinking about all the female flesh that would fill them. No big sizes, just small and medium, for the perfectly formed. And at five guineas a pair, high-toned. I imagined long, lithe bodies encased, framed by the fabric, a lovely quiet swishing sound as the panties were slipped on or off. I washed my hands all the time, it only seemed right. I pressed the silk to my cheek, buried my nose in it. I fell in love with a pair of panties. I was

3

in heaven.

And at school, I stayed in the D stream.

Two O levels. And one of those only came at the fifth
attempt. I sat it in June, then again in December. Then the
following June and the following December. Finally they got
so sick of seeing my name they just gave it to me. French. I
was bilingual. A failure in two languages, the bane of my
mother's life. What would the neighbours think? How they
would gang up, and with malevolent relish seize the disas-
trous outcome of my school career as a tool to torment her
with, winking and nudging one another as she passed,
waiting at gateposts for the chance to scoff.

'How's your Ned doing, Mrs Selby?' one of them would
ask.

My mother would struggle for words, mutter excuses and
run. Inside, she would close up the curtains as though
someone had died.

'Ned, Ned,' she would say, wringing her hands. 'How
could you let your mother down? Two O levels. Is that all the
thanks we get for years of scrimping and sacrifice, for
threadbare carpets and broken furniture, just so's we could
send you to school? Only two! What will people say when
they find out? Why, even the fat boy on the corner has ten!'

It was chastening, but what could I do? Her shame was so
great I didn't understand. Then finally, after three days of
enforced blackouts, even I started to wonder what people
would say.

'Here comes Ned Selby, he of the two O levels!'

'Only two! Good Lord, I feel sorry for his mother!'

'How many O levels have you got, Selby? Two! Is that all?

4

Even the fat boy on the corner has ten.'

Pretty soon I'd get that fat boy once and for all. He was called Falmer. At school I used to punch him just because he was fat. Now I had another reason. Ten O levels.

'Fat Falmer, get the dogfish out of the formaldehyde tank, will you? Falmer, kill the worms, will you?'

Then he'd roll up his sleeves, and avidly do it. Two minutes later he'd be chewing his nails, plunging his hands into whatever wretched cadaver was pinned out in his dissecting tray. He was unsavoury, but he had ten O levels.

Well, all that was behind me now. Fat Falmer, headmasters and dogfish. I left the Minister in the living room amidst all the heart-rending evidence of sacrifice – the home-made lamp standards; the wall-to-wall nylon carpet, thin as a sheet, peeling away from its rubber base, the rubber breaking up and leaving black droppings where you walked; the smeared sofa; the radiogram with the back off; the old TV whose picture rolled. Old things, run down things, broken things. Eloquent accusatory things. I choked as I went upstairs, gripping the chipped banisters. It was all my fault. I was scum. An ungrateful cur. A wastrel. My poor mother, so easy to please. All she'd ever wanted from me was polished brilliance, awards on speech day, enough O levels to count on the fingers of two hands. She wanted to be able to hold her head up with pride, in a room full of fat boys' mothers. Had that been so much to ask? No, of course it hadn't. I slumped on my bed, riddled with guilt and remorse, surrounded now by evidence of all that had distracted me from the proper goals and ambitions of a school-boy. There, stacked next to my precious Pye Blackbox, was the root of the trouble, my records, a whole collection spanning the musical tastes of half my life. At the back, long since relegated to obscurity, Trad Jazz; then Benny Goodman, my big band era. Brubeck next, and finally the glorious present: Errol Garner, the MJQ, Jimmy Smith, The Jazz Messengers, Ray Charles. These were all piled up at the front, charged suddenly with blame for having deflected me from the straight and narrow. I could see Errol grinning manically out from the first cover, elegant in immaculate tuxedo, poised to play merry hell with all conventional proprieties. April in Paris? Certainly!

On a shelf was my Brigitte Bardot scrapbook, pictures I knew by heart, indelibly etched on my mind's eye. Brigitte at seventeen, eighteen and twenty. Brigitte looking demure in a tutu, sultry in a gypsy costume. Brigitte looking achingly sexy and fresh in a white bikini. That mouth, always a little open. That arse, firm and high without a trace of overhang. Pictures lovingly pasted into an old school notebook, flattened out gently with all due care and devotion. Once I'd heard that her sister was studying English at a language school in town. I didn't know which, but I'd lurked outside one for days, searching for family likenesses, preferably that arse or that mouth, hoping for just a glimpse of something approaching the real thing. I didn't see anything close, of course, but it didn't matter, I still had my pictures. I could be alone with them. I could be alone with her.

'You shouldn't have time for girls until you've finished your education.'

That was the clarion call which rang through the house for years from one or other of my parents. They meant sex, needless to say. I wondered whether I could now make a legitimate claim that my education was over. Would the family finally relax? With only two O levels, I doubted it. I reached up for the notebook, flicked through the well-thumbed pages, gazed at the vision therein. Ah, sex. And jazz! Brigitte and Errol, two flames which swept through family life.

I could remember exactly when I first got burned. At least by the flesh. Music had always been there. Who knows, I might have burst out of the gate to the magic of George Formby's 'When I'm Cleanin' Winders', it just developed, but sex, I could pin that down to a night, a breast roughly handled, a nipple tweaked in the darkened upstairs room of a friend's house.

It was an innocuous party: parents home by eleven, beer, and the kind of games which involved ritual though irreproachable grapplings presaged by only the briefest introductions. Somewhere there are faded photographs of that party, fresh faces barely recognisable now. I'm wearing a trilby three sizes too big and look ridiculous. It kept flying off as I cycled to my friend's house, the wind catching under the brim, all the passing motorists laughing, me still sublimely unselfconscious waving delightedly back, tipping the hat which I had to hide under a jacket to get out past my parents. I was invulnerable, fourteen and a half, and oh so sophisticated.

It turned into a momentous night, despite its fierce restrictions. That breast beating hotly under my sweaty adolescent palm changed everything. Chemistry, Physics and the rest were never the same again. I did away with all such childish things to pursue the breast unfettered, and the thigh naked.

And eventually made it, of course. With Susie, a golden

girl of miraculous thighs, warm as oven-fresh bread. I couldn't believe my luck. How come I'd been singled out? I was nothing special to look at. I had short legs and a long body, bits and pieces of my mother and father that didn't seem to hang together. I had my mother's ears and my father's nose. On her you didn't see them, for they were hidden in luxuriant hair. On me they were bright red and slightly translucent. As for the nose, it was thin, bony and long; inclined, I thought, to give my face a fleshless, pinched appearance. But I must have had something. Something rare, something subtle. Nobility of mind, perhaps. Generosity of spirit. For Susie was *she*, radiant on the threshold of womanhood, a vision, a dream. Brigitte stepped down from my pictures. I wanted nothing less than to swim through her flesh, to bask in it, to wallow helplessly, weeping for joy at the beauty and wonder in all things.

We'd had it arranged for days: a date, a place, equipment bought. Several times an hour I'd tap the package nestled next to my heart in my breast pocket. Three? I'd need all of those, and then some, the way I felt. I was excited to the point of panic, spurting with anticipation. Tap, tap. Yes, it was still there. Wonderful, I was grown-up at last. People knew, I could tell. On the street they nodded respectfully, passing a man of the world. Tap, tap. Oh boy! Only two days to go.

But suppose my mother noticed! What a wailing and a howling there'd be then. What a tugging of the hair.

'I should have known, I should have known,' she'd cry dementedly. 'I've seen your scrapbook, I've heard your jazz. I knew it would come to this. I prayed it was just a phase. You'll get her in trouble. What will the neighbours say? Oh, think of the shame! Wait till your father comes home . . . '

'Mother, mother! I'm sorry,' I'd howl, breaking down. 'I

won't cause any trouble, I promise. I'll tear up my book. And here,' I'd add, offering the package from my pocket. 'take these . . . '

Devastating images rendering me suddenly limp and nauseous.

But how could she possibly know? You couldn't tell from a look. Surely that was a myth, a tale invented by old wives to sabotage fun. No, I resolved confidently, my mother had no way of knowing.

Tap, tap. That's more like it! Zero minus one day. Yippee!

Incredibly the day came, then the evening. We cycled to the spot, the place where everyone went who was unmarried, too young, or for some other reason living at home. *The* spot, a meadow of long grass and reeds skirting the river near Grantchester. What a splendid evening it was. Enchanted even. Birds sang, gnats gathered. We locked up our cycles, walked hand in hand. I waded through long grass in a trance. I couldn't speak. Susie looked lovely, a red dress, hooped petticoat and stiletto heels: fresh, unworried, matter-of-fact. Suddenly there was a grunt beside us, a man getting up.

''Ere, you watchin' us?'

He was a giant with slicked back hair, fighting a zip on the tightest drainpipe trousers I'd ever seen. I pushed Susie forwards.

'Who, sir? Me, sir? No, sir . . . not I, I'm down here for the same purpose you are . . . just looking for a place to get started . . . '

'Cos if you bleedin' are, I'll tear your fuckin' eyes out . . . '

9

Perhaps we could call the whole thing off. It wasn't too late. It would be for the best, really. But no! What was I thinking of? Susie tugged me away. Tap, tap. We lay down. Then there was the rolling down of her roll-on. In those days everything rolled on or off, unravelled, burst or spilled. Oh God, the tops of her tan stockings, a glimpse of thigh, tufts of hair. Well, what did I expect? I didn't know. It was all too marvellous.

'Susie, Susie . . . I'm I'm . . . sorry . . . '

I wasn't. I felt great. I snickered, I preened. Did I, Ned Selby, really do it? The signs seemed to suggest so. I could actually do it. It worked.

'My God, did anything split?'

A voice I hardly recognised cut through my euphoria:

'It didn't get a chance!'

Susie was snapping on her stockings, definitely not preening, not snickering . . .

'Whatsa matter?' I said.

The first of many such utterances, such questions.

Ah, Susie. She was never one of the family's favourites. Apart from anything else she'd disrupted my education. I'd been obsessed with her, a hopeless drooler, anxious all the time that if she left it would be a very long while before I got to sow *any* oats again, let alone any wild ones. She was the 'wrong' sort, which is precisely why she was absolutely right, and why, too, she didn't stay long with me. I mean, I didn't exactly get the hang of it. For six months she put up with my urgent fumblings, then ran off with an Italian. I suppose he knew better what to do, though, God knows, Susie might have given me a few helpful hints. Had she grabbed my hair just once when I was down there sucking and slurping as if in desperate mouth-to-mouth resuscitation, shifted my head an inch with a few words of well-meaning advice – 'Not there, for Christ's sake, *there*!' – it might have made all the difference. Anyway, she didn't. In the end it was all a matter of luck. Another time, another place. Hitting the spot. My God, what was that? Better do it again!

Now there was Agate, a nice girl who was, my father said, much too good for me. I think he wanted her for himself. She was deferential and pleasant, thoroughly harmless, the perfect girl-next-door except that she lived on the other side of town. It was a strange name. Her old man carved wood for a living, travelled by moped, and wore long hair. He also played the oboe. Her brother played the flute, her sisters played the violin and the cello, and her mother thumped out tunes on the piano. Agate herself played the French horn. They were a pocket orchestra. They had musical evenings, the whole family united in song, all blowing and bowing and hammering away enthusiastically. They drank wine at meals, went camping abroad in summer and came back with tans, olive oil, and with the girls clutching photos of dark-haired boys with smouldering brown eyes. They said 'ciao' instead of goodbye and, when they weren't making music, spoke to each other in Italian or French. All very tiresome.

The first time I saw Agate she was stepping out of a boat onto the bank of the river. It was summer and she was wearing blue shorts. All I could see were her thighs. I thought they were wonderful. Actually, they were. But she

11

had varicose veins on her calves, and no ankles to speak of. In these she took after her mother. Her mother was knock-kneed, and had long red hair, usually pulled back and fixed in a tight plait. She spent most of her time reclining on a sofa, a harridan with a loud, booming voice and a quick line in bitchiness. Oh, she was special! And she hated me. Naturally. I was fucking her daughter.

Agate was training to be a nurse. Three nights a week she'd come over to my house. We'd sit with my parents, my father in his chair, my mother in hers, the two of us ensconced on the sofa, chatting inconsequentially, watching TV. Then my parents would go to bed. As soon as I heard their light go off, I'd be on her, throwing her skirt up over her head, peeling down panties, taking her from behind. By now I was tired of her moon face, her varicose veins, but she still had a fine big arse, and I'd pummel away at it for a couple of minutes, smother a bellow and let rip. Then we'd dress and I'd cycle back to the nurses' home with her, feeling depressed. I didn't like the ride, but there was always a rapist about and my father would have killed me if she'd pedalled back alone and come to a sticky end.

Our relationship was just dragging on, the way they sometimes do, an institution. But I was bored, bored, bored. I wanted new excitements, especially now I was into my last six weeks of freedom. I didn't want attachments to tie me down. I didn't want to explain anything. I wasn't married. I wasn't old, though in that sitting room I sometimes felt as if I was. As I lay on my bed with the incomparable Brigitte in my hands I decided, not for the first time, to give Agate the push. She'd be sad, I knew. I was already sad. But she'd get over it. After all, she was much too good for me. I'd exercise my generous spirit, leave the way clear for a better person. I got to my feet, found 'Concert by the Sea', and slapped it on

12

the turntable. Then I lay back: 'Autumn Leaves'. All at once I was in Carmel, in a church overlooking the ocean. There was no Agate, no O levels, and no jobs. Just Errol grunting at his bass player, me and two thousand others offering ourselves up to the transport of his wild and swelling chords.

2

How could I even have thought about dumping Agate? Didn't I realise how lucky I was? She was kind, thoughtful. She looked after sick people. She played the horn. Besides, what would I do without her arse? I had Brigitte, of course. On paper, anyway. But I was still growing. Every once in a while I needed to sink my teeth into something real.

These were my thoughts a couple of nights later when Agate came over. My father was lecturing us, warming to his favourite theme, a variation of 'what this country needs'.

'Bad management,' he was saying. 'Oh yes, I see it all the time in my line. And traditions. We're sunk over our heads in traditions. Old equipment, old ways, it's just not in our nature to abandon them.'

I glanced at my mother. She was straining to hear the TV, which had been turned down so that no one would miss

14

these pearls. Then I shifted my position to face Agate. Either she was listening intently, or putting on a mighty good show. She was nodding gravely. Encouraged, my father sped on.

'Now you take the Yanks . . . '

He glanced over his half-lenses, stabbing the air with a finger. A potential captain of industry, thwarted only by a lack of educational opportunity. A manager, a chairman of the board, a financial wizard with the touch of gold. Governments, whole states might have depended on his decisions. A shake of the head here, revolution there. Power, money, machines, all might have been his.

'Yes,' he finished, 'that's what it boils down to.'

In silence we pondered his words. He sat back, from time to time looking at each of us. My mind was a complete blank. I struggled to find an appropriate response. Anything that didn't contradict him. Preferably something that would bring the proceedings gradually back to the mundane.

'Anyone for a biscuit?' my mother put in suddenly.

I could have hugged her.

'I'll make the tea,' I offered at once.

The end was in sight. Tea, biscuits, close-down, lights out, wallop. It was a tradition. Oh dear Lord, I gave thanks for traditions! I couldn't wait to get stuck in, way over my head.

Agate had come by straight after her shift. She hadn't even bothered to get out of uniform. She was immaculate, still wearing her watch on a pin over her left breast. All she'd changed were her surgical stockings which she used on the wards to support her legs. Now she was wearing a black pair, with a delicate lacy pattern. How thoughtful that was! How utterly and totally considerate. She was a credit to the National Health Service. And I was a sick person desperately in need of her merciful attention.

I hurried back with the tea. I started slurping it down,

15

furiously dunking digestives in an effort to speed everything up. It made no difference at all. It was all very measured and polite. I began to suspect my old man had a malicious streak. Since he fancied Agate himself, he was dragging this out.

I snuck a look at my watch. Agate had to be back in her room by twelve. It was just coming up to eleven. Twenty-five minutes for the ride, that still left forty. More than ample for my purposes.

The last biscuit eaten, cups gathered and cleared, they finally went to bed. I waited on tenterhooks for the light, holding my breath. Click! I was on Agate in a bound, a sort of body roll, sideways, straight on to her lap. Nothing wrong with that, I did it all the time. But I sensed something was up. No eager compliance. No avid lips. All I found was resistance.

'Whatsa matter?' I asked, my hands twitching to pause as I rolled back. 'Whatsa matter?'

'Nothing.'

'Nothing? What do you mean, nothing? Get 'em down then. It's a tradition.'

'That's just it,' she said. A bubble was bursting, I could tell. 'Old ways . . . '

I thought I was hearing things.

I looked at my father's empty chair, half expecting to see him nodding at me over his spectacles.

'For Christ's sake, don't listen to *him*,' I begged. 'He's just jealous.'

'Who?'

'My father.'

'What's he got to do with it?'

'Everything.'

'Don't be ridiculous!'

16

'Ridiculous! You've just come out with his very words. He's poisoned your mind with all that bad management shit. Look, we've only got half an hour . . . '

I started rolling again. Again I was stopped.

'I'm tired of all this,' she began.

That's what you get for having nice thoughts, I thought. I'd lost the initiative. Weakly, a last-ditch effort, I said, 'I've been looking forward to this.'

'That's the point,' she said, shaking her head. 'I haven't. You're just using me. For . . . for this. We never go out.'

I seized what she'd offered.

'Well, what would you like to do?'

'That's not what I mean. Listen, Ned, I've just started work. I like it, but it's hard work. I want some fun. We're not married, we're young. But sometimes in this room I feel we're exactly like your parents. Just waiting, filling in.'

Now she was criticising my folks. She had no right.

'Don't you say anything about *them*,' I shouted. 'They sacrificed everything. Look at these lamps, these chairs. I suppose you think you're too good for me. You and your fucking horn.'

That told her. But she came right back.

'I'm not talking about them. I'm talking about *us*,' she said.

'So am I,' I snapped indignantly. 'And if we're not coming, we're going.'

I jumped to my feet. I marched out of the room and out of the house. I opened the garage, wheeled my bike to the path and then waited. It was starting to rain. Agate came to the door. As she put on her mac, her uniform rode way up to her thighs and I felt a pang of regret for my impulsive departure. Perhaps we could start over again from lights out with just a little more delicacy on my part. I checked on my

17

chances with a lightning perusal of her face. They were at absolute zero. Her mouth was set, her lips sloping down in an expression of grim resignation.

No sex, and the prospect of a wet ride. It wasn't my night.

'It isn't my night,' I grumbled impatiently, one palm turned up to the rain.

'You don't *have* to come,' Agate obliged.

'Oh no?' I grunted. 'And what if you get raped? How would I live with myself?'

'You'd find a way,' she said icily.

This wasn't the girl I knew. The one I knew was kind and considerate and didn't answer back.

'What's that?' I asked.

'You'd find a way,' she repeated. 'I don't suppose it would bother you much.'

Would it? I pedalled in silence, speculating.

'There!' she said pointedly. 'You were supposed to say you'd be distraught.'

'I'd be distraught,' I replied. As a matter of fact I'd feel as guilty as hell. Such a nice girl. A nurse! A horn player! My father would kill me.

Agate had pedalled into the lead, and I put in a spurt to get abreast of her. There was no sense in courting trouble at this stage, though what with the rain it seemed an unlikely night for a flasher to be about in. Yet you never could tell. Despite a soaking a clutch of nurses and their boyfriends were locked in wild embraces outside the nurses' home, greedily sucking the last dregs of excitement from the evening before time was called. Usually Agate and I did the same. Only the week before, in fact, when we were still in love. Now when we dismounted we stood awkwardly separate, bedraggled in the rain. I could tell it was over. It wasn't what I expected, and I felt at a loss. Shouldn't one of us

18

throw some sort of scene – start wailing, remember old and good times, exchange a memento or two? We just stood there, holding our bikes.

'Better get in,' Agate said finally.

'Yes,' I said.

Neither of us moved.

'Well . . . see you,' she said.

I nodded. Suddenly, the whole of our lives together flashed before me – musical evenings, discussions involving the state of the nation, varicose veins, tea and biscuits. I looked lovingly at her nurses' watch, gripped by nostalgia.

'Thanks for everything,' I managed.

'I wouldn't have missed it,' she said, considerate to the end.

'Give my regards to your parents.'

'And mine to yours.'

We were strangers already.

'Goodbye, then.'

'Watch out for the rapist.'

She turned and went in, not even bothering to wave from the doorway.

I stood watching for a moment, then got on my bike and rode home in the rain. I felt terrible. She played the horn. She had a fine big arse. She was far too good for me.

For two days I didn't know what to do. I moped. I hung around the house. I felt sorry for myself. I spent hours in my room listening to mournful music. Agate was a part of me, a precious part, a limb. Without her I limped, off kilter. Every time I closed my eyes I saw her: in uniform, out of uniform; in shorts, out of shorts. I saw her moon face, her soft eyes. I saw her horn.

My parents were wonderful, supportive to a T. When I didn't get up the next day, my mother came into my room to roust me. She took one look at my face and stopped in her tracks.

'What's wrong?' she inquired, poised between panic and genuine concern.

I shrugged.

'Something is wrong. I can tell.'

I nodded heavily from the pillow.

'I knew it!' she cried, her voice quavering in panic. 'It's happened, hasn't it?'

I nodded again, turning to face her.

'Oh my God!' she moaned, a hand going up to her mouth. Once there, she bit it hard, flinching with a deep intake of breath.

She started to babble.

'What'll we do? What'll the neighbours say?'

I'd risen up on my elbows, but I flopped back the moment I realised what she was thinking. Sod it, I thought, she can think what she likes. I let her dance for a while, doing nothing to relieve her. She sat down, she got up. She bit one hand, then the other. She glanced at me, then turned quickly away as if suddenly scalded.

'I can't even look at you,' she exclaimed. 'Think of the shame! Her poor mother . . . such a nice girl. Not like that . . . that . . .'

'Susie,' I helped.

'Susie,' she repeated, flinching again. 'How could you do it?'

'Do what?' I asked. We'd have this one out properly.

'You know . . .'

She started to shake.

'Don't think we haven't heard you when the lights go out. In my own living room! I told your father it would end in tears.'

'It's not what you think,' I said, after a pause.

My mother gasped. A little colour drained back into her face.

'You mean. She's not . . . not . . . '

'No!' I snapped angrily. 'We've broken up is all. I've lost the love of my life is all. And I must tell you how much I appreciate your fine words of comfort.'

But she didn't hear me finish through the tumult of her relief. She dropped in my chair, exhausted, mumbling thanks, praising the Lord.

I got up, and went to the bathroom.

The old man was no more consoling. He sat through supper in silence, his eyes unable to meet mine. Another grievance to add to the list. I felt his own disappointment almost as acutely as I did my own. Never to see Agate again! Something good had gone from both our lives.

Half-way through pudding his exasperation spilled over.

'Ach,' he said, throwing his spoon down. 'Ach, she was much too good for you.'

'I know,' I burst out. 'Don't tell me, I know. I've ruined my life.'

'You'll never find her like,' he added. 'She was kind. She was thoughtful . . . '

'She played the horn . . . '

'An angel!'

'Yes . . . '

'You're a fool . . . '

'Yes . . . '

'Two O levels.'

'Yes . . . '

'A drifter.'

'Yes . . . '

'Six weeks!'

'Agh . . . '

To hell with Agate. Two days of this and I was back in the sea where there were plenty more fish.

The Crucible was a scene from my mother's worst nightmare. Its very existence was an affront to her sense of decency. It had puddles of booze on the floor, sawdust, a juke-box, tarts, queers, and American servicemen. There wasn't an O level in the place. I loved it. It had noise, laughter, foul language, and outbreaks of random violence. It was a place where you could cadge drinks from the queens, ogle the tarts, and get cut-price fags from the Yanks.

I spent more and more of my evenings there. But it was becoming expensive. I had no pocket money now I'd left school, which was all part of the six-week master plan to force me into gainful employment. A full week had passed. I was still ahead by a nose, but it hadn't been easy.

This night I was on my uppers. I paid the last of my cash for a small beer, counting out the change in pennies and halfpennies I'd rifled from coat pockets all over the house. Then I sat down, sipping slowly. It was early. Except for a gaggle of girls, the bar was empty. These were the camp followers, the nieces of GI brides, instantly identifiable by their turrets of backcombed hair, pastel-blue outfits, and high white stilettos. All powdered and puffed and preened, they were doing their best to look like Elizabeth Taylor. Except for Pam, almost a dead ringer, most of them failed miserably.

I tried to clock Pam, but she wasn't interested. I was too young, too un-American and too broke. I watched whilst she and a friend waddled and giggled their way to the juke-box, marvelling how they always had to do everything in pairs. How would it be to hump that, I wondered. Scary, I guessed. Everyone knew about Yanks. They had big cars, big wallets, and big wangs. So be it.

The Four Seasons sang out. 'Rag Doll'. The girls waddled back to their table.

'Well, Ned,' I said to myself. 'What you have here is a cash crisis.'

'I know,' I agreed.

'So let's go about this logically. What are your realisable assets?'

I thought for a moment.

'A Pye Blackbox. Some records. But I can't possibly sell those. They're my whole life.'

'You're in trouble, then.'

I nodded despondently. There had to be something else. A scrapbook. A used dissecting kit. A packet of three. That is if I sold it before Jan. '76. I couldn't think of a worthwhile thing. Then it hit me.

'Golf clubs,' I cried jubilantly. 'I can sell my golf clubs.'

'You'd never get away with *that*!'

'Don't *you* start,' I said. 'Why the hell not?'

'What would old half-lens say? He had big plans for you. Ambitions.'

'He knows I don't play any more,' I protested.

'And *we* know what he feels about it. You could have been

23

a champion, a new Arnold Palmer.'

'A fate worse than death,' I sneered. 'My man was always Sam Snead.'

'All right. A new Samuel Snead. You were a natural. What on earth made you stop anyway?'

'Sex,' I said instantly.

'Sex?'

'Susie,' I added.

'Hmm . . . That Susie again.'

I sighed at the memory.

'If you ask me Susie has a great deal to answer for.'

'Oh, I don't know,' I said wistfully.

'Golf for sex?'

'A small loss for a large gain is how I see it,' I answered.

'Explain *that* to the old man.'

Promptly I did. Well father, when it comes right down to it, that is, the heart of the matter, when it comes to a show-down, the little man in the boat or the hole in one, I have to go for the former.

'Ach,' I could hear my father respond.

'Maybe you're right,' I continued, re-engaging myself.

'Of course I'm right. It looks like being a job then.'

I contemplated my fate. Here I was on the verge of manhood, no money, no girl, staring a job in the face. All it needed to make my evening was for Agate to come waltzing in, with a radiant grin on her face and Dr Kildare on her arm. A doctor! Christ, he'd have more O levels than the fat boy on the corner! Aghast, I spun round. I stared at the door expectantly. 'I told you so' began to ring out in my ears. I could see my father shaking his head.

Plenty more fish in the sea? Who was I kidding? I hadn't seen Agate for over a week and I hadn't had even a nibble.

24

Maybe I should call her up, ask her over to my house. Old ways, it just wasn't in my nature to abandon them.

I smiled as that line popped into my head.

Maybe the old fellow was right. But I'd show him.

3

Come the second Friday I didn't have enough money to visit the jazz club. I couldn't even raise five bob. It was pathetic. I'd stripped the chairs, done the coats and the drawers, and for three days I'd walked everywhere with my eyes fixed on the ground. Nothing, not even a measly sixpence. I was desperate. The club was a must, a rite. I felt bereft without it. I was a regular, my face just beginning to be acknowledged by all the right people. I had taste, I knew music. I nodded in all the appropriate places. I grunted appreciatively during solos. Oh, they could tell I had rhythm. Once, when I'd requested 'Autumn Leaves', the bassist had said:

'Yeah, we can do that.'

And then they'd done it. Imagine! I was a friend of the bass player.

'It's my favourite number,' I'd said.

He'd turned to the rest of the combo and repeated my line. The drum player performed a neat little roll with his brushes. The tenor man honked out a riff. The pianist peeled off a scale. I was in with the band! My enthusiasms raised them to previously unscaled imaginative heights.

And now I was letting them down. Because I couldn't come up with five bob.

I'd tried everything. For two nights I'd cadged drinks in the Crucible, hoping to run into the American major. But the old cocksucker wasn't about. Where was he now when I badly needed some change? The toad, with his gruesome plaid jackets and phoney correspondence degrees! It was sickening to think of the times he'd squeezed my leg under the table for only an occasional vodka and tonic. He owed me! Next time I'd take him for a real ride. Accept his gifts, then skip before he had a chance to get serious. Beat the old bastard up. Inform the authorities.

I'd tried buttering up May at the local record shop. Usually she was good for a ticket. But not this time. She was going through one of her more frightened, tentative phases. I couldn't even get close. The management was keeping a check. So was her boyfriend.

It was a game we played, except for an occasional ticket or trade discount, one that was without end or outcome. I'd go into a cubicle to hear an album, and after a while May would get in beside me. We'd gaze at each other, then kiss. All of a sudden she'd push me away, overtaken by guilt.

'Whatsa matter?' I'd ask.

'I mustn't,' she'd say. 'I'm going to be married.'

'Not yet, surely,' I'd grumble.

'Soon,' she would say.

'Three years isn't soon.'

'Someone will see us.'

27

'Who?'

'One of his friends.'

Sometimes we'd meet up after her work, and walk down by the river. Before long the same thing would happen.

'Don't,' she'd say.

'Why not?' I'd ask.

'Someone's bound to be watching.'

I'd turn quickly to look. I'd squint hard along the way of her finger.

'I don't see anyone.'

'I think it's his aunt.'

'His aunt!' I'd exclaim.

'Please, I must get back.'

It was a harmless flirtation, picked up, put down, never followed through. Both of us knew it, accepted it, enjoyed it. We were from two different worlds. She was a shop-girl loping towards marriage. I had two O levels. I was destined for wonderful things.

Though not, it seemed, for the jazz club.

That night I cycled into town anyway, still vaguely optimistic. You never knew. Something might turn up even at such a late stage. Maybe I'd see my friend the bass player. Perhaps he'd say:

'Hi Ned, good to see you again. Why don't you come in with me? Someone like you shouldn't have to pay for a ticket.'

On the off chance I set out early. I locked up my bike some distance away from the hall which was situated above May's record shop, then I lurked in the alley skirting the side entrance. I felt good in my yellow shirt with the button-down collar, ready to grunt in all the right places.

A girl ahead of me knocked and was ushered in. She wore a scarf over her hair, dark glasses and a zip-up leather jacket. I could tell at a glance that she knew music. She was one of the select few, someone like me who didn't have to pay for a ticket.

A van drew up at the end of the alley. I began ambling towards it, wondering what I should say. 'Hello fellas' or just, 'Hi, man' to the bass player? I'd never used that greeting before, though I'd heard it often enough. 'Hi, man. What's happening, man?' I said it over and over, trying to get accustomed to it. But it just sounded odd in my ears. In the end I simply nodded. I didn't think anyone had noticed what with the dark and their preoccupation with numbers and solos, but a voice called 'Hi' from behind me, and I turned to respond, 'Hi, man' on the tip of my tongue. Luckily that's just where it stayed. The girl with the scarf had come back outside. She was obviously well in with the band, one of the few on 'Hi, man' terms. I bit the tip of my tongue, did my best to saunter casually round the corner of the alley, then headed for home.

'Hi Brigitte. Hi Errol,' I said once I was back in my room.

'Hi, man,' they returned instantly.

Next morning I woke from the middle of an unpleasant dream. I was in a concert hall, in the best seat, dead centre of the front row, waiting excitedly to hear my old friend Errol play the piano. To begin with I was the only person in the place, but the doors opened and it quickly filled up with hundreds of fat boys, all of them clutching paper scrolls. I looked around me. There wasn't an empty seat in the house.

29

Suddenly the lights dimmed, the curtains on stage drew aside, the fat boys cheered and waved their scrolls. There, beside a piano, stood Errol, wearing a mortar board and a scholar's robe. After a moment he turned to the wings. I couldn't believe it: Agate walked on with her horn. Pandemonium broke out. The audience whistled, using their scrolls as trumpets to increase the volume of noise. At the height of this horror a fat boy, Falmer, the one from the corner, approached me.

'You're sitting in *my* seat,' he said.

'No, I'm not,' I replied nervously. 'I'm in with the band.'

'Where's your ticket?' he demanded, poking my chest with his scroll. 'Here's mine. I've got ten of them.'

'I'm in with the band,' I repeated. 'I don't need a ticket.'

The fat boy turned to the stage.

'Errol,' he said. 'Hi, man.'

Errol smiled broadly and waved. Then he sat at the piano, adjusted his robe, and peeled off 'Autumn Leaves'. The fat boy grunted appreciatively in all the right places. Two bouncers escorted me out just as Agate began her solo. I looked back over my shoulder, my eyes fixed in a desperate appeal. She didn't miss even a beat.

I woke up in a cold sweat.

And that's when it hit me. Freedom was all very well, but when you were broke it was nightmare. I hated to concede even an inch to the Minister of Ag, yet the conclusion I'd just come to gave him the best part of a mile. It would leave him gloating for months.

'Six weeks,' he'd say, sniggering a little over his specs. 'How many did you manage? One? Or was it two?'

I'd stick two fingers up. Sharply, angrily. Then he'd say:

'So, my lad, what are you going to do with your life?'

Then it would be my turn.

'Please don't misunderstand me,' I'd say. 'I'm not thinking about a career. I'm merely considering a holiday job. Something to tide me over while I examine my opportunities.'

'Huh,' he'd guffaw. 'You've had all the holidays you're going to get. And the opportunities . . . '

'Don't tell me,' I'd interrupt. 'I could have been another Arnold Palmer.'

'Now you'll just drift. Why, when I think of the opportunities you've had! If I'd had just half of them I'd have been a captain of industry by now, a manager . . . '

It would be a short step from there to his state of the nation speech. Couldn't he get it through his head that I wasn't interested in bad management? I was of an artistic bent. I was good at English. I wasn't a fat boy.

I lay in bed feeling depressed. Usually it helped to think of something warm and wonderful – Brigitte's arse, even Agate's, Susie's certainly – but my attempts this time made me feel even more sad. I was assailed on all sides by the great issues: money, sex, Arnold Palmer, fat boys, jazz, freedom, loneliness, jobs. Why wasn't my family rich? If I had to be born, why wasn't I the son of a captain of industry? I didn't ask to go to that damn school but since I'd gone why hadn't anyone recognised my musical talents and taught me the bass? Or even the horn? God, it was tough being seventeen. Life had only just begun but it was over already.

'You must eat,' my mother fussed at breakfast.

'What's the point?' I moaned.

I went on aimlessly stirring my cornflakes.

'It's the calcium in the milk,' she said. 'It's good for your bones. They're still growing, you know.'

She could be kind when she wasn't concerned about neighbours. And she'd been a beauty in her day. I often wondered how my old man had won her.

'No, they're not,' I said mournfully. 'My life's over and all you can speak of is calcium.'

'What would you have me speak of, dear?'

I sighed heavily.

'Loneliness, freedom, money,' I recited.

She laughed a slight, awkward laugh.

'I don't know as I can,' she said. 'I leave all those complicated matters to your father. You should talk to him. When he was your age . . . .'

'He was never my age,' I snapped, raising my voice. 'He was too busy being thwarted.'

'Thwarted?' she asked.

'Yes,' I said. 'In his effort to be a leader of men.'

'You'll never understand how difficult it was,' she protested.

'I've been told often enough.'

'There was the depression . . . ' she said.

'And the war. Don't forget about the war.'

She looked at me, shaking her head.

'Loneliness, freedom,' she said softly. 'We didn't have time to think of such things. We had to get on with the job. It doesn't do to think of such things.'

'I can't help it,' I said sharply. 'I went to a good school. I've got two O levels.'

She winced at my last remark. For a moment I expected her to launch into the fat-boy-neighbour routine but there was a short silence while she gathered herself. Then she said:

'Life's over, indeed! In five years you'll most likely be married and settled in a nice job. By then *you* won't have

32

time to dwell on such things.'

There was a smile on her face, a forlorn smile that gave her words all the features of a plea. It shook me so much that I stifled the cry of alarm the instant it rose in my throat. At that moment I couldn't rob her of hope. Marriage, a nice job! It just wasn't in her nature to abandon them. I smiled forlornly back, then did the only thing I could think of. I ate my cornflakes. They'd gone soggy, but the milk had calcium in it and calcium was good for the bones. I knew mine were still growing.

In town, half an hour later, I felt absolutely wretched, but I couldn't pin down what was actually bothering me. A welter of thoughts and feelings buzzed through my head. One minute I wanted to put everything right: in one fell swoop give up jazz, scrapbooks; go to night school for as long as it took me to be a captain of industry; start hitting golf balls again. In the very next the mere prospect of such a course of action gave me the willies. The right thing always turned into the wrong thing.

I mooched along the river, walking the Backs. The fucking Backs! Just then I couldn't wait to see the back of them. Suddenly it seemed to me that they'd governed the whole of my life. All those spires, those lawns. Each one a rebuke, reeking of O levels. Every time I looked up I expected to run into my old headmaster.

'Selby, isn't it?'

'Yes, sir.'

'What are you up to now?'

'I'm thinking of going to night school, sir. Study to be a captain of industry.'

'With two O levels! Don't be absurd! Look around you, boy. Prizewinners down every street. What hope do you have?'

'I went to a good school, sir.'

'But you wasted the opportunity. You're a fool, boy.'

'It's not too late! It's never too late. I'm destined for wonderful things.'

'Ach.'

Sod him. Sod 'em all. What did they know? They knew nothing of Brigitte, nothing of Errol. Why, they wouldn't know 'Autumn Leaves' from the fat boy on the corner.

I began laughing to myself. How stupid could I get? I'd let everything become jumbled up in my mind. It was all so simple really. A plus B equals C. It didn't take a maths O level to work that one out. A, no pocket money, plus B, no work, equals C, no nothing.

I walked on in the direction of the city centre, reviving with every step. I felt the defiance come coursing back, flowing through me like the blood in my veins. This is more like it, I thought. I felt a new bounce in my stride. For a while there I'd lost sight of my priorities. True, I was broke. True, I was loveless. True, my relationship with the bass player seemed to have suffered a slight hiccup. But these things were only temporary. Life wasn't over by any manner or means. The main thing was to organise, take one step at a time. So far I'd been side-tracked. The old man had driven me into *his* corner. It wasn't a matter of concessions. By trying to prove him wrong, I'd only made him seem right. The crafty old devil knew exactly what he was doing, setting me up. It was humiliating to be broke, also restricting. Under the circumstances a chap might be driven to kowtow completely. Well, I'd learned my lesson. I wanted a measure of independence. No more Mays, Majors, or maters. Suddenly, I knew where to get it. I couldn't think why it had never occurred to me before except that I'd resisted the whole notion of work. Now what I had in mind was virtually all fun. It would give me high profile, social contacts and cash.

I quickened my step, elated. For the first time in two weeks I knew what I wanted to do with my life. The machine! I wanted to work the machine.

The owner was busy in the office so I sat in the basement waiting for her to get through. Nothing had changed. There were the same shell ashtrays that spun if you knocked them, scattering ash all over the tables, and the same red tomatoes for the ketchup. It was just like being at home. Except for the spot by the river Susie and I had done most of our courting here. I couldn't remember the number of times I'd given her a grope amongst the plastic vines and wooden grapes. This was the El Sol. For five months Susie had been my moon.

Susie!

The memories came flooding back, a great tidal wave, swamping me. She was an orphan. No mother, no father. For her I'd tried to be both, but I didn't get much of a chance. I was just getting the hang of it all when she ran off with the wop. What was it? The dago lilt in his voice? His smouldering brown eyes? He had fair hair, which is unusual for an Italian. It was because he came from the north, she'd said.

The last I heard, she was engaged to a farmer. Not fat Falmer, of course. But a man of the soil.

Ah, Susie!

It was here I first touched your thighs. In this seat. At this table. Oh, holy seat, holy table. I shut my eyes in worship, offering silent thanks. My fingers gently traversed the formica. It was sticky with coffee and cake crumbs. How dare they spill coffee, I wondered. Didn't they know this place was a shrine? I pulled out my handkerchief and polished hard. I rubbed and rubbed, then I spat and rubbed some more. It was the least I could do. I was just finishing off when the office door opened.

She was a good sort, the proprietor. And she listened without making me nervous. I wanted a job, I said. I was honest and clean, I said. She studied my face, then suddenly snapped her fingers. I nodded, wondering just how much she remembered, then I stroked the formica for luck and she asked if I could work the machine. The machine! She was asking if I, Ned Selby, could work the machine. I mumbled I couldn't, but said I could easily learn. She said someone could teach me after the lunch-time rush. Meanwhile, how did I feel about washing-up? Dreadful, I thought. It wasn't at all what I had in mind. Washing-up was way out at the back where you couldn't ogle or be ogled. It was dirty and hot, hardly a fit start for someone destined for wonderful things. How much was the pay? I asked. Five shillings an hour, she said. Five bob! The price of a ticket! I accepted at once.

Mission accomplished. I gave thanks at my shrine, then made my happy way home.

4

On first sight Andy was a real smoothie, but he had two O levels, knew jazz, and he worked the machine. I'd seen him around for years. In fact, in those distant pre-Susie days, his Arnold Palmer had been second to my Sam Snead in the local boys' golf championship. Later, I'd run into him at the roller rink, but his high leaps and triple turns cut a considerable dash, putting him in a different league from me and my monotonous stumbling circuits. On the scale of good looks he rated at least a ten, and with a ton of upper-crust charm he gave the impression that butter wouldn't melt in his mouth. Naturally, the impression was false. Three days into my training, he confided his system: lunch times, just keep the till open, ring up only half the orders, keep a check on the rest, then pocket the difference. Already he was a captain of industry, without doubt destined for wonderful things.

We hit it off almost at once. More than anything else he had style. He wore tinted glasses, a leather jacket with proper lapels and a vent at the back, drainpipe jeans, and snakeskin winkle-pickers: all those things my folks wouldn't have me seen dead in. What was the secret, I asked him during an afternoon break.

'Well Ned,' he said slowly. 'I hope this won't alter your attitude towards me, but you're looking at the product of a broken home.'

'No!' I exclaimed.

'Yes, I'm afraid so,' he said. 'And as you can see it has blighted my life. It's all right for you chaps with devoted parents. You don't know what it's like to get what you want without a struggle. I mean, I've had it easy.'

I shook my head in mock sympathy.

'That is awful,' I said.

'Isn't it?' he agreed. 'I've only had to ask and it's been given. I don't know what it is to yearn. What's it like, Ned?'

'Terrific,' I answered. 'Life wouldn't be the same without a good yearn.'

'That's just what I thought,' he said. 'All this time I've been missing out. I'm underprivileged, deprived. I'd feel sorry for myself if I only understood how.'

'You shouldn't make too much out of it,' I told him. 'Lots of people have overcome the same handicap and carried on to live totally disappointed lives.'

'I'm not optimistic,' he said.

'I think I can help out,' I said. 'Why don't we swop jobs? You wash up and I'll take over on the machine. You might find it instructive.'

'I appreciate your point, Ned. But it simply wouldn't be fair. I wouldn't wish my unfortunate lot on anybody. As you say, those of us who come from broken homes should bear the burden manfully. I'll do my best, you can rely on it.'

He got up, smiling broadly, and walked back behind the counter to serve a customer. I watched him work the machine, brewing coffee with untrammelled verve and swagger. It was obvious there'd never been a fat boy on the corner of his street. It was inconceivable. A life without fat boys!

In the kitchen amongst the mountains of smeared crockery, I yearned. For the rest of the day I gave it all that I'd got. Boy, I was good at it. What scope my yearning had! What vision! I yearned for this, I yearned for that. I was a master of yearning. I wasn't selfish. I included everybody. My yearning was noble, a gift to the world. I yearned for all those who didn't know what it was like to yearn. I yearned for tomorrow. I yearned for today. My yearning knew no bounds. I yearned for carpets. And lamps. I yearned for the thwarted. For Errol. For Brigitte. And that's not to forget Susie. It was almost religious, my yearning. I yearned for all the big issues. For O levels and winkle-pickers. I yearned for an absence of fat boys.

I went home yearning.

'How was your day, dear?' my mother inquired.

'All right,' I replied. 'I yearned.'

Her face fell. Despite all the problems, she wanted her son to be happy. Now I was in trouble, yearning for things I couldn't have. How had she failed me?

'What for?' she asked fretfully.

'For shoes,' I said.

'Shoes?' she repeated.

'For snakeskin winkle-pickers,' I said wistfully.

It was a red rag to a bull. Instant anger, instant panic, as though a switch had been thrown.

'Not in this house, no! Over my dead . . . wait til your

father comes home.'

'Forget it,' I said. 'They belong to a friend.'

'A friend,' she burst out. 'What kind of people wear shoes like that?'

'Andy,' I said. 'You remember the golf . . . '

She lurched to a chair, moaning.

'Oh my God, not him! His mother's divorced. She has boyfriends. He's had everything he wants. I'll speak to your father.'

The Minister seemed ready to let that one pass. He was concentrating on a different tack.

'How's the job?' he asked hopefully.

'Wonderful,' I said. 'The start of a glittering career.'

'Strains your intelligence, does it?' he went on, undaunted by my breezy tone. 'Taxes the full range of your intellectual achievements?'

'Oh yes,' I replied, seizing the advantage. 'I bring method to it. I'm the thinking man's washer-up. I wash up in two languages.'

'Ach,' he said disgustedly. 'When I was your age I wanted to make something out of myself. Your generation doesn't know what it is to struggle. You've all had it far too easy.'

I started to smile.

'What are you grinning at?' he snapped.

I paused, looking him straight in the eyes.

'I spent the whole afternoon yearning,' I said.

It was the light at the end of the tunnel. The ray of hope. Four days of washing-up had concentrated my mind after all those holiday jobs had failed. His face lit up. He was beside himself. He'd been right all along. I was coming around.

'Ned,' he said, his voice suddenly tender with affection and pleasure. 'I'm happy to hear it. Proud even. Perhaps you're growing up. Perhaps the years at school weren't wasted after all. What were you yearning for?'

Bingo. I had him.

'Shoes,' I said. 'Snakeskin. Very long, very narrow.'

'Ach,' he growled. 'Ach.'

Hi, Errol. Hi, Brigitte.

It wasn't such a bad life, after all. At least not now I had five shillings an hour coming in. Suddenly I was a man of substance. I could sit in the Crucible, buying drinks with a flourish.

What would you like to drink, Major? What's that? You just obtained another degree? Marvellous. How many does that make? Ten! Good Lord, a magical number. No, I didn't say anything about fat boys. You must be hearing things. Let me buy you a drink to celebrate.

No, of course not, May. I've come to see *you*. Whatever makes you think I want a ticket? I can buy my own ticket. How about a walk by the river? Oh, I see, somebody's watching. Yes, you already told me. Soon, you're going to be married.

Five shillings an hour! Not a king's ransom, but it jangled in my pockets. And the work was easy. The only busy time was immediately after lunch when the tables were littered with mugs and plates and I'd have to sweat for an hour to catch up. After that it was a doddle, with plenty of time to sit

41

at the staff table socialising. I still aspired to the machine, of course, but Andy had that nailed down. He was saving hard, taking terrible risks with the till, breaking his own rule that the only safe time to keep it open was during the midday rush when nobody had even a moment to check what he was ringing up. I didn't know what he was saving for, only that he was urgent about it. Then one day he was late in. I was on the machine, beginning to get the feel of it, when he appeared.

'Shit,' I told him. 'You might have waited till I got through lunch. I was about to try out your system.'

'Don't worry,' he said. 'Soon you can have it. I've got what I want. Let me show you when we get through.'

Come six o'clock, after we'd closed, I followed him along the street to a parking place beside one of the college forecourts. I spotted it at once. It was beautiful. It was compact. It was light blue. It was feminine, with sexy bulges on each side over the back wheel.

'Wow,' I said. 'A Vespa.'

I circled it, touched the seat, ran my fingers across the immaculate paintwork, gently pulled at a brake lever.

'What do you think, man?' he asked.

'Man, it's beautiful,' I said. The word tripped naturally off my tongue. Man. I barely even noticed it. It fitted, all of a sudden felt smooth. If only the band could have heard me.

'How about a spin?' he asked.

'You bet. But what about the L-plates?'

He went to the front, and the back, ripping off the two emblems, stuffing them deep inside his jacket.

'What L-plates?'

Man, how grand it was to be young and free and on the back

of a brand-new baby-blue Vespa! The whole town opened up before us, then rolled away behind. Girls gaped. Women nudged their children to look. Andy and Ned, destined for wonderful things! We cut through the traffic. We bounced along cobbled streets. We tore up the open road. Ned and Andy. Enemies of fat boys everywhere. Look, oh do look!

'Like it?' Andy asked.

We'd skidded to a halt on the gravel drive of a smart detached house a couple of miles from the centre of town. His mother's, I guessed.

'Like it?' I said. 'It's "Concert by the Sea", it's . . . '

'"Thelonius at the Town Hall!"'

'"Jimmy Smith at the Baby Grand, Wilmington, Delaware!"'

'It's "Sketches of Spain".'

For two or three minutes we went on in this vein, exhausting a list of favourite LPs. Common ground! Who cared about a broken home? We were united in jazz, speed and O levels.

We went straight to his room at the top of the house. It wasn't just a bedroom, but a proper bed-sit, with all the amenities. I was amazed. Apart from the bed, which was bigger than your average single, it had two easy chairs, book shelves, a desk, a huge closet for clothes and, I could hardly believe my eyes, an electric hotplate. Straight away Andy put coffee on. He had his own pot, mugs and milk. There was a small wash basin in one corner of the room, a hi-fi of course, and a big stack of records, which I nosed through at once. All those we'd mentioned outside were there, and a lot more besides. Stuff I'd heard of. Stuff I hadn't. 'Poetry and Jazz'. That was a new one on me.

'Poetry?' I said scornfully.

'It's great, man,' he said. 'I'll play it later.'

I stood up, and made a quick tour. On the desk was a sheaf of papers and an old office typewriter. A sheet of paper jutted out of its roller. I read a couple of lines of print:

> Her nipples erected
> Like a box of sandwiches

What on earth did that mean? I read them again, none the wiser. Andy answered my unspoken question.

'Surrealism,' he said. 'You know, Dada.'

I didn't. But I nodded. Of course, yes!

'That's from my book of dreams,' he went on. 'I write down all my dreams. I got the idea from Jack.'

'Jack?' I echoed.

'Jack Kerouac,' he said.

Must be one of the foreigners Andy knew from the El Sol.

'Author of *On the Road*,' he said. 'You must have read *On the Road*?'

'Well . . . yes . . . no . . . I think I picked it up once.'

The coffee boiled, and he poured me a cup. I let it cool a little, then sipped it gingerly. Tea was my drink. But this was something different. This was nectar, the best coffee I'd ever tasted, smooth, dark, grown-up coffee.

'It's French,' he said, again reading my mind.

This was a whole new world. Poetry, dreams, French coffee, Vespas. Whatever next, I wondered.

A door slammed below us, then a voice called:

'Andy, darling, you home?'

'Up here, Judith,' he shouted, then to me said: 'My mother.'

'But you called her Judith,' I said, shocked.

'That's her name,' he replied. 'Don't you call your mother by her name?'

I shook my head. Christ, for a moment I wasn't even sure if I *knew* my mother's name. What the hell was it? Anne? Jane? Dilys? Mary! That was it. I tried it out in my head.

'Hello, Mary.'

'Up here, Mary.'

No, I decided, it just wouldn't work. Neither of us would ever get used to it. I couldn't go around calling my mother Mary. After all, she *was* my mother. Come to that, I was her son.

'I usually just grunt,' I told him.

That wasn't the end of it, by any means. There were more surprises to come. His mother knocked – knocked on his door, then waited to be invited in. It was *her* home. I assumed she paid the bills, yet here she was waiting for his permission to enter.

Then there was the way she looked. She didn't look like a mother. Not my idea of one, anyway. She had fair hair billowing over her shoulders, a full mouth with lipstick applied, and she wore fashionable clothes. Stiletto heels, and a light summer two-piece showing off good legs and a full figure. She was well spoken, with a low-pitched voice and, most amazing of all, she smiled a lot. I tried to estimate how old she was and finally put her somewhere between twenty-five and forty. She shook my hand, with a grip surprisingly firm, then she and Andy exchanged a few bits

45

and pieces of domestic information. I was relieved not to have to talk to her. Not that she was unfriendly, far from it. But she was a combination of things which I found unsettling. Maybe my mother had primed me. Here was a woman who unquestionably had boyfriends.

After she'd gone I asked Andy about the nature of their arrangements. The knocking, did she always do that?

'Of course,' he said, as if it was the most natural thing in the world. 'She has her room, and I have mine. What we do in them is our own business.'

'You mean, she lets you have girls up here?'

'Certainly. That's why she knocks. I don't think she wants to see me at it.'

I shuddered. Awesome images flashed in my brain. My mother. Me. Susie.

'No,' I said. 'A thing like that in my family would make several people desperately unhappy.'

He couldn't see it, and I didn't try to explain. It was probably a function of economics, or of class, or of thwarted educational opportunities. I don't think even I understood. All I perceived was a difference. And it made me green with envy.

I didn't say anything about that either. We spent the rest of the evening listening to jazz, and drinking more coffee. But I also made mental notes, a whole bunch of them for future reference. I was a working man, nearly eighteen. It was high time my people responded.

5

Pay day!

How I loved that little brown envelope with my name on it! Inside were two five-pound notes, two pound notes, and some loose change. Sometimes I got one five and seven singles. It didn't make any difference to me. As long as it all added up to the same. Twelve pounds.

I knew exactly how I was going to spend it. I had it all mapped out, down to the last penny.

I went straight to the big department store where I'd once worked amongst the panties. I knew domestic appliances were on the first floor, next to hardware. I walked up to the counter and rapped it confidently, a man with money in his pocket.

'I want the latest in electric hotplates,' I said. 'No expense spared.'

'Ah, you must be a student, sir,' the assistant said. 'We

cater to a lot of students.'

'Yes, my man. You could say I was a student. A student of life. Something of a poet, too.'

The assistant looked at me blankly. A grey man in a khaki coat.

'Surrealism,' I explained. 'Dreams.'

'I recommend the single-bar Belling, sir,' he said.

The single-bar Belling! Yes, it had a good sound.

'A fine model,' he continued. 'Guaranteed to last a lifetime.'

I sighed heavily.

'A lifetime? How long is that? 'Tis but the winking of an eye. All flesh is grass.'

'If you say so, sir.'

'I'm not interested in lifetimes,' I said. 'Only in today.'

'That's probably wise, sir.'

'Does it come with a plug?' I asked.

'No, sir, you have to buy the plug separately.'

You philistine, you ignoramus. You don't know it, but in one line you've summed up the angst of the age.

'I'll take it,' I said. 'How much with the plug?'

'That'll be one pound, seven shillings and eight pence, sir.'

It rolled off his tongue, sheer poetry.

I paid the cash, delving into my brown envelope. I wasn't proud. I was a working man. A washer-up. A poet amongst washers-up, certainly, but after all one of the people.

'Thank you, my man. Wrap it up for me, will you?'

In this manner I did the rounds. Soon I was fully equipped. I bought a coffee pot, two mugs. I bought coffee, sugar and

milk. Then I made my way to the nearest bookshop. I found
Fiction, and went straight to the Ks. Kerouac, Jack. There
were several volumes, which I examined at once. I picked
out two with the most promising covers, illustrations of half-
naked girls, with racy blurbs: 'zany antics of America's
young beats in their mad search for kicks'; 'crazy mixed up
novel, about frustrated youth going nowhere fast'. I reckoned that would just about do it.

I hurried home with my packages. I'd spent five pounds,
but every penny had been worth it. My room was no longer
just any old room. It was *the* room, transformed by my
purchases into a salon. What beauties would grace it in the
future! What wits!

I was so proud of my single-bar Belling. I watched its wire
element glow. It hummed gently, a cheery sound, hopeful
and optimistic. I listened, then put on the water. I watched it
while it heated, bubbles steaming up to the surface, tiny at
first then huge, with a great glugging noise. I spooned out
the coffee, one for each person, and one for the pot. Just like
tea. I let it brew for a while, the smell filling my room,
pervading the whole house. Then I poured out a mug.
Cheers Brigitte. Cheers Errol. Christ, it was something to
savour. My own coffee, in my own room!

I was deliriously sipping when my mother burst in.

'Something's burning up here,' she shrieked. 'What on
earth have you done?'

Why not, I decided. Give it a try.

'Mary,' I said, pausing to emphasise my use of her name.
'It's merely my coffee. Perhaps you would care for a mug?'

It sounded strange in my ears, but I managed to keep my
control. I didn't foam at the mouth or bleed from the eyes.
Nor did the ground open up and swallow us whole. Still, it
felt like a close run thing.

'Mary?' she murmured. 'Mary?' As though asking a question. She looked at my Belling, then at me, then back at my Belling.

'Yes,' I said. 'It's part of my new regime.'

Suddenly she was stricken with terror.

'Regime?' she asked timorously.

I nodded.

'I'm a working man. A grown-up. I claim my just deserts.'

'Just deserts? What do you mean, just deserts?'

'You know what I mean. Coffee in my own room. Visits from friends. Privacy.'

'What friends?' she asked sharply.

'Any friends,' I replied.

'I know what friends. Girlfriends is what friends.'

And she was off. Neighbours. Shame. Fat boys. A nightmare vision of sex, jazz and mayhem, exposed to the whole street. She fled from my room. My mother. I didn't see how she could ever be Mary. Marys were young and unworried. They wore lipstick and fashionable clothes. They had boyfriends and smiled a lot.

All right, so I'd have to revert to the grunt. But I still had my Belling. I poured more coffee, and stretched out on the bed. Then I reached for my books.

I didn't read much as a rule. There were books in the house, plenty of them, but the Minister didn't go in much for stories. Stories were like girls as far as he was concerned: not things you messed with until you finished your education. I'd long since given up trying to find the fun in *Science for the Citizen* or *Maths for the Millions*, and the novels I'd studied at school had had the fun completely knocked out of them. I simply wasn't prepared for what followed. I opened *On the Road* and was hooked from line one. I read for seven straight hours. I didn't just read it, I lived it. I *was* Sal Paradise, and Dean Moriarty. I *was* on the road, zipping between all those exotic places. I didn't eat, I didn't sleep. I just drank coffee after coffee, getting bug-eyed on caffeine and kicks. I parked cars, I hopped freights. I listened to jazz, I ran between girls. I grunted appreciatively in all the right places. Reading, I felt exactly the way I felt when I listened to my favourite music. I was taken up in it, whirled around, momentarily dropped then whisked away again. On, on, into the morning. I finished the book as the sun came up, then I went back over it, picking out scenes I remembered. The ride across Nebraska with the blond farm boys and Montana Slim; George Shearing at Birdland; the wild Mexico run. Something had clicked in my brain. I was exhausted. Exhilarated. Replete. I went to sleep singing. Thank you, Andy. Thank you, Jack. Oh thank you, man!

When I woke up that afternoon I was a beatnik. I didn't look like one. Not yet anyway. I glanced at the mirror and the same old face peered back. A clean-shaven face with red ears and a long nose, but I was a beatnik all right. I'd been one all along without realising it, without knowing the word, without understanding there were people out there, lots of them, with the same restless poetic soul as mine, scorning the same conventions, engaged in the same mad search for kicks.

I put my coffee on. My Belling hummed into life. I checked downstairs. The Minister and his wife were out, probably at golf. I laughed out loud. Golf! A game for squares. They were teeing off unaware of their son's zany antics. I put on jazz. Oliver Nelson. I opened the windows, threw them wide so the neighbours could hear. What do you think of that, squares? Like it? Of course you don't. You're too bowed down with jobs and kids and payments and TV. Well, loosen up. Listen!

I went out for a walk, clutching a notebook in case I had visions. Perhaps I'd hitch into town, just stick up a thumb and go wherever the first car to stop was going. Maybe it would be a beautiful woman, a beautiful rich woman who'd want to know about my philosophy of life, who wanted kicks and jazz and sex.

I got to the end of the street. Coming towards me was Dan Dean, the terror of the village. He was six six, lean as a beanpole, but tough with it. He didn't so much walk as lope. Crepe soles on his shoes as thick as a sponge cake, jacket as long as an overcoat with dinky little velvet lapels. Nobody had told him Bill Hayley had come and gone. Nobody had told him anything. Ever.

'Hi, Dan, man,' I said.

I heard myself say it and thought: Oh Christ, no, don't push your luck. But it was already out of my mouth. There was a moment when he looked as if he would pounce. Then he smiled. And nodded. He was an outlaw like me. And, of course, it takes one to know one.

I walked on, through the grounds of the nearby women's college. A few of the girls were out on the lawn in the sun, smearing oil on their bodies. I sat down by the pond and observed the ceaseless bobbings of the moorhen. Ah, life! Teeming, restless, without purpose. I got out my notebook. Something would come to me, I was sure. I sat waiting. A few minutes passed. Nothing. I waited some more. Still nothing. It was certainly disappointing. If I was going to have a vision, this was the place for it. You couldn't force these things though. The point was to be spontaneous, to empty the mind, then let it happen. I tried not to think of anything. But it was impossible. I kept thinking of oil-smeared bodies, taking sly peeks. The girls were only two or three years older than me, but I knew we were separated by convention and many O levels. Still, I was certain there was one amongst them, restless and questioning, who strove to explode the habits of tradition and authority. She'd be expecting a sign. I doodled in my notebook. Soon she would sidle up, look over my shoulder.

'Ah,' she would say. 'A scribe. I could tell.'

I'd smile, then nod my head ever so slightly.

'What are you writing?' she'd ask.

'Poor wee lines,' I'd reply, 'scarce half made up.'

'May I see them?' she'd venture.

I'd smile engagingly, then say:

'I'm afraid they're unfinished.'

But she would plead. Then I'd recite:

> 'Her nipples erected
> Like a box of sandwiches.'

Nodding thoughtfully, she'd say: 'You are influenced by surrealism, Dada.'

'Of course,' I'd say, responding to the inevitable. 'You know about such things.'

Then we'd talk about art and life and jazz and kicks. At last she'd invite me for coffee.

'There's a single-bar Belling in my room,' she'd tell me.

'A fine model,' I'd respond at once. 'Guaranteed to last a lifetime.'

'I'm not interested in lifetimes,' she'd explain.

'I know,' I'd say. 'You're only interested in today.'

53

Then we'd take each other's hand and get to our feet.

I doodled for all I was worth, occasionally glancing up to scan the lawns. Nobody moved. Girls were reading, smearing, chatting, but definitely not searching for signs, or striving to explode the habits of tradition. What was the matter with them? Didn't they realise there was more to life than tans and O levels? I wanted to walk among them distributing copies of *On the Road*, to tell them about Sal and Dean. But something about the lawns and the spires stopped me. Then suddenly it struck me. A sort of vision. I was alone, ignored because of my attitudes, my soon-to-be-unshaven appearance. I couldn't expect acceptance, recognition for flying in the face of everyday behaviour. Scorn, yes. Fear, yes. Why, Dean, Sal, Andy and I were part of a new heroic breed of individuals, more like gods than men, whom other men would therefore fail to comprehend.

All right girls, I thought as I prepared to leave, it's your loss. Go your blinkered, herd-like way. I stood up, red ears, long nose, notebook. I was magnificent. One of the few. Dean would have been proud of me. So would Sal.

'I want a word with you, my lad,' the Minister said when I got home.

'I shall be in my salon,' I said. 'Making coffee. You have sugar and milk?'

He winced. The half-lenses slid down the reach of his

nose. His eyes popped.

'Word! Here! Now!' he stammered, poking my chest with a finger. 'No coffee. No salon.'

I waited.

'What's this I hear about just deserts?' he asked.

'Ah, you've been talking to Mary,' I said.

'Mary?' he snapped. 'You mean your mother, don't you?'

'I mean your wife,' I said.

'That's what I said,' he said.

'Yes,' I said. 'Mary.'

'And that's another thing,' he said. 'Since when did you start this Mary business?'

I pondered a moment.

'I think it was yesterday,' I said. 'But as I'm only interested in today, it is hard to determine.'

'You're getting too cocky, my lad. I'm heartily sick of your antics. And so is your mother.'

'Mary, you mean.'

'Ach,' he said. 'I'll give you a just desert. You cook in your room, it's a lodging house. It's a lodging house, you pay rent.'

Then he smiled and held out his hand.

'Five pounds a week,' he said. 'As of today.'

The old bastard, I thought. But for the sake of appearance I managed a grin.

'Hardly a king's ransom,' I said as I dipped in my envelope and drew out the last fiver.

He took it at once, turned his back and walked away. I went upstairs to my salon. There was my Belling. My coffee. There was my jazz, my books. Hi Sal, hi Dean. Hi Errol, hi Brigitte. I felt almost sorry for the old fellow downstairs. He was thwarted and trapped by traditions. He thought he'd beaten me. How could he, a mere mortal? He was dealing with gods.

I laughed. I made myself some coffee, rich French coffee. Then I picked up the other Jack Kerouac and started to read.

6

I was sitting at the staff table during the lull after the lunch-time rush the following morning, trying to give Andy some idea of the situation.

'I don't believe it,' he said.

'It's true,' I said.

'Rent, you say?'

I nodded.

'Incredible,' he said.

He shook his head in sympathy, then his face suddenly brightened.

'Still, there's one good thing,' he added.

'Oh yeah, what's that?'

He looked at me, grinning steadily.

'Well, now that you pay for it, it's officially yours. You can do what you like in it.'

'Hey, I hadn't thought of that,' I said.

'You can move the girls in.'

For a few joyous seconds I imagined the whole thing. Wild scenes, naked girls. Buckets of coffee. Then I considered the prospect. It was all very well in theory, but in practice I envisaged a snag.

'I don't know about that,' I said. 'Mary and the Minister would still be downstairs knowing what I was doing, and I'd be upstairs knowing they knew. The whole house would be throbbing with tension. I'm sure I'd be in a fit state.'

'You'd soon get used to it,' he said, laughing confidently.

I wasn't so sure. But I agreed anyway. Five pounds did give me some rights. And the right to have visitors was definitely one of them.

'As for the money,' Andy said. 'I'll let you have two lunch times a week on the machine. That should be ample time in which to pick up a fiver. Plus a little bit extra besides.'

I just stared at him, speechless with gratitude.

'Oh, wow, man. That's great,' I gushed.

He was Dean to my Sal. Or Sal to my Dean.

'Just don't fuck up my system by getting caught out,' he warned.

It was poetry in motion, the pure magic of style. I wished I could see myself. I was quick. I was versatile. I was fluid. I never spilled a drop. I felt I'd been born to it. I was Dean Moriarty of the coffee machine. Thank you, madam. Can I help. you, madam? I saw respect in their eyes. Sometimes desire. My white jacket was spotless, crisp with starch. My smile was radiant. A word here, a joke there. No room for complaints.

'Excuse me, I don't think you rang up the price of my

order.'

'Why no, madam. That's because I was in error with somebody else's. I'm just tallying up.'

Florins, half-crowns. The pockets of my coat bulged. Soon I jangled with change.

Then there were girls. Foreign students, come for the paellas and pizzas. Sultry Italians with lustrous dark hair and deep voices. French girls, aloof and elegant with pungent cigarettes and shapely legs. Blonde Brunhildas with pale blue eyes and hearty appetites. Oh, come, all ye faithful. Bonjour, guten Tag, volare. No, please, have this one on me. Do you like jazz? Kicks?

'Vat are zeze keeks?'

'Ah, if only you knew.'

'You tell me, ja? Is gut für mein Englisch.'

'Of course. Only too happy. You must visit my salon.'

'Salon is room, ja?'

'Ja, is room mit ein Belling.'

But they weren't interested in me. They wanted money and cars, nightclubs and cha cha. It was a shame. They were exquisite, exotic, svelte, but they were all squares. They'd never had to hitch a ride, or hop a freight. They didn't know what it was like to yearn. Still, I kept on making my pitch. Most of them didn't even notice. It was crazy of me to consider them, but I couldn't help myself. How long had it been? Weeks, years since Agate. These faces would haunt me for days, these bodies for nights.

Then, near the end of my shift, it happened. A plate of paella paid off. She was foreign, ja. She was blonde, ja. She was exquisite, nein. But she sat by herself, not one of the crowd. Beauty was a nebulous conception anyway. Skindeep at the best of times. We beats were more concerned with the inner self than with outward displays.

She smiled from her table, inner self luminous with passion. I smiled back, my best lopsided grin flashing beacons from my generous spirit. At the first opportunity I walked over, and sat down.

'How was the paella?' I asked boldly.

'Gut,' she said.

I'd made a fine start.

'You must be from Germany,' I offered.

'Ja,' she said brightly. 'I come from München. My name is Martha.'

The way she said it the th was hard.

'Martha from Müchen,' I said, for some reason thinking of Eskimo Nell. 'That's almost a poem.'

She laughed, shifting a little with pleasure.

We were moving along rapidly. Geography, art, this was going to be easy.

'I write them myself,' I said.

She looked at me questioningly.

'Poems,' I told her.

She thought that was marvellous.

'Say me a poem,' she said. 'Vun of your own.'

I decided it was too soon to give her the old box of sandwiches routine. I'd save that to impress her with later. I searched through my memory for any old piece of verse. At last I came up with a line:

'I must go down to the sea again.'

I could tell I'd scored a big hit the moment she started to bounce up and down.

'I love ze sea,' she burbled excitedly. 'I love ze swimming. I love ze tan.'

Oh Christ, I said to myself.

'How about the cha cha?'

It was her last chance. Intently, I scrutinised her face. If it

60

had shown any sign of delight I would have been off, back to the kitchen. She shook her head emphatically. Thank God for that. Then she floored me.

'Ze twist. Ze peppermint twist,' she said.

She performed a gruelling motion with her body, a sort of squirm, with her elbows and shoulders beating the air. People were beginning to look. I prayed Andy would stay out back, at least for the time being.

'You like to dance?' she asked.

I nodded half-heartedly, giving it only cautious approval.

'Gut,' she clapped. 'Ve go dancing, ja?'

Jesus, I thought, a live one. I could just see her, wearing an embroidered blouse and suede shorts, woollen knee socks with little green tabs on the garters, marching through the Austrian Alps with her plaits flying, every so often letting out a spine-chilling yodel.

'Yes, we can go dancing,' I said. 'But first I want to know more about you. Your hopes, your dreams. What you want to do with your life.'

'Ach,' she said, with the first hint of impatience. 'You und your poems. You zink too much.'

She sat up in her chair, pouting huffily. Our first quarrel. But it didn't last long. Soon she was smiling again.

'I zink you are romantic, no?'

'No,' I blurted. 'Absolutely not. Don't get me wrong. I'm a restless youth going nowhere fast. I'm amazed you can't tell. I live for today. For kicks.'

'Vat is ziz keeks?'

It was my turn to get huffy.

'I'll tell you one thing it isn't.'

I paused for effect.

'Vell,' she said. 'Tell me.'

'The fucking peppermint twist.'

It burst out of me, perfect timing. It didn't faze her a bit.

'I don't understand,' she said.

'Of course you don't. Only a select few of us are able to understand. A new breed of heroic individuals who scorn the world of Chubby Checker.'

At the mention of that name her eyes lit up, and her elbows and shoulders beat the air again. I was beginning to like her. At least she had spirit, vitality. Maybe all she needed was a nudge in the right direction. It wasn't her fault she was German. Somewhere in there was an inner self desperate to get out.

'Listen,' I said. 'Do you know Jack?'

'Jack?' she asked.

'Jack Kerouac.'

'I don't know anyvun,' she said. 'Only five days hev I bin here.'

'No,' I said. 'He's a writer. A god. He wrote a bible. The beat's bible.'

She frowned at me.

'You are Catholic, ja?'

My voice rose.

'No, for Christ's sake, I'm beat.'

'But you believe in God, ja?'

'Ach,' I said. It was the first time I'd ever used that expression in my life. It took me a moment or two to recover. I sucked in a deep breath.

'I believe in Dean,' I said. 'Dean and Sal. The heroes of *On the Road*. That's a book. A book by Jack. Jack Kerouac. About young beats on a mad search for kicks.'

'Vat *are* zese keeks?' she demanded. 'Vy don't you tell me if I don't understand?'

All right, I thought. I'll give her both barrels.

'Sex,' I said.

62

I don't know what I expected exactly. Something like my old girl's reaction to that word. A shudder. A moan. Lips turning blue. Not a bit of it. A demented sort of laugh. Then she brought one of her hands down hard on the table. I jumped.

'Ha,' she said, eyes gleaming. 'Is zat all. Vy ze mystery? Sex is normal, ja.'

I thought she was going to bite me. I leant back, nodding vigorously. Perhaps it *was* in Bavaria. In my neck of the woods it was mostly fraught with imminent peril. I couldn't believe my luck. I'd only been on the machine three hours, yet here I was with at least five pounds of loose coins in my pockets and with Martha from München avid to get at my body. The weekend was beginning to shape up nicely. Thank Christ golf was an all-weather sport. Nothing short of a typhoon would keep the Minister from his Saturday game. That would give Martha and me a safe five hours for coffee, jazz, maybe even a twist or two. Ample time to get down to it. It wouldn't do to rush her on our first date.

Date? I was running away with myself. I hadn't even asked her out. That was the difficult part. In the space of a few seconds I tried the question fifteen different ways, a whole gamut of possibilities, all to myself. Suddenly I was tongue-tied. It was pathetic. He who worked the machine. Proud owner of a single-bar Belling. Jazz lover. Scholar. For Christ's sake pull yourself together!

Her knees scorched mine under the table.

Say something!

Anything!

Try to imagine how Dean would do it.

'Would you like to come round and listen to my records?' I babbled at last.

Jesus, not that!

'You can always bring your own.'

Worse.

Her hand slapped the table again.

A god, Selby? A child. A worm. The lowest of the low.

She was preparing to leave, laughing.

'Ven?' she asked.

I thought I was hearing things.

'Ven shall I come?' she asked again.

'Saturday,' I said quickly.

'Gut,' she cried. 'Ve hev fun, ja?'

'Ja,' I managed. 'Ve hev fun.'

Just then I didn't think I was capable of giving her precise directions out to my place, so we arranged to meet at midday, there in the El Sol. With that out of the way she promptly left. Then everything started to seem a little unreal. I went to the staff table and sat down. Could I have imagined it? Martha. From München. The peppermint twist. It was quite possible. I drank a coffee, smoked a cigarette. Then I started to come round, a warm adult feeling. Ned Selby, King of the Beats. I felt pretty damn pleased with myself.

The week was ordinary after that. I'd obviously peaked early. I did another lunch time on the machine and by Friday I'd easily covered my rent. That night I paid the Minister two weeks in advance, just to keep an edge. Upstairs I counted out ten quids' worth of small change then I dumped the coins in his lap as I was preparing to leave the house. He didn't like it a bit. A few of the coins rolled on to the floor, and I went after them, stamping. That was a mistake. I had on Andy's snakeskin winkle-pickers. They were hard to miss anyway, but as I danced after the money they really let rip, belting out that old refrain 'Lock up your Daughters'. Mary cowered in a corner, gasping stuff about divorcees, friends and bad influences, whilst the Minister glared furiously over his specs.

'Where do you think you're going, my lad?' he demanded.

His mode of address was beginning to irritate.

'Out,' I replied briskly.

'Not in those, you're not.'

The shoes were already part of me, an outward expression of my inner self. For a moment I'd no idea what he meant. He jabbed a finger in the direction of my feet. I looked down. Ah, yes! There they were. There I was. Beautiful.

'These?' I questioned. 'Mes chausseurs? Meinen shoesen? Why on earth not?'

'Because I say not,' he said.

'What sort of reason is that?'

'All the reason I need.'

'These aren't just shoes,' I protested.

'No,' my mother bawled, disgust mingling with the fear in her voice. 'They're pointed. Snakeskin. Yellow.'

I swung towards her.

'Yes, that's true as far as it goes,' I said airily. 'But you're only looking at outward displays. There is that within which passeth show. We must learn to look *beneath* the surface, find the essence at the heart of all things.'

My mother turned to the Minister.

'I told you,' she said. 'It's that Andy. They're *his* shoes.'

'No, Mary,' I said, shaking my head with infinite condescension, 'if they express the inner self of he who is wearing them, they belong to the wearer.'

'You're not going out in them,' the Minister said again.

'I am.'

'You're not.'

'I am.'

'You're not.'

Stalemate.

I wondered whether other beats had this trouble. To have to smuggle a pair of shoes out under my coat and change in the street was a betrayal of the whole ethos. Was I a part-time beat, a weekend beat, or what? What would other beats say?

It was humiliating. But I had to make a decision. I was already late for the club. Tomorrow was Saturday. Martha from München day. I didn't want anything to go wrong with that. Forcing the issue might have some drastic effect on my arrangements. I looked at my mother, twitching in her corner. She might take to her bed. Break down. Her short game might go to pot. They'd come home early. I'd be caught at it.

I rushed upstairs, and changed into my regular slip-ons. I put the snakeskins into a bag and tossed them out of the bathroom window on to the front lawn. There was a thud as they hit the ground, but nobody ran out after them. It was clear the old fellow thought he'd won another round. When I reappeared he checked my footwear, then gave me a sly, humourless wink as I went out the door.

I picked up my package from the lawn and walked to the bus-stop, disappearing behind a hedge to change shoes along the way.

Either my inner self was in a very bad state or the shoes didn't fit for by the time I got to the club the damn things were pinching my feet. I could feel something oozing down there. I still had the package with my slip-ons in it and I thought about changing back, but I reckoned I'd be all right once I got to a table. Luckily, the band's early session was in full swing, and nobody noticed my painful arrival. I gritted my teeth, bought a beer at the bar, and limped to a table near the bandstand. I sat down, glancing quickly around. When I was sure nobody was looking I undid my laces and kicked off the shoes. The relief was exquisite. I started tapping my feet. Gradually the music washed over me. I shut my eyes, drank my beer, and just let my mind wander. Images swept in and out of my head but all the while I kept in touch with the music. I was happy. For as long as the music played it was the best of all possible worlds.

For three hours nobody yearned and nobody was thwarted. I grunted and moaned at my table, thinking of Dean and Sal with Shearing at Birdland, trying to remember what Jack had written. It was something to do with a moment, the moment when everything is about to arrive – that moment when you know all and everything is decided for ever.

Yes, that was it . . . but it was over too soon. I opened my eyes. My glass was empty. The bass player had zipped up his bass and walked to my table. He was bending down to pick up the shoes.

'Don't forget these,' he said, smiling wryly.

Perhaps we were friends again.

I took them from him and forced them on to my feet. Then I walked to the door. They still hurt like hell. Outside I changed into my slip-ons, hobbled to the nearest taxi-rank and got a cab home. It was beginning to rain. The start of the first typhoon in British meterological history.

Shit!

67

7

What with my sore feet and the pounding rain I didn't get much sleep. All night I kept thinking of Martha. Would she turn up? Probably not, I decided. By now she was mixing with her own kind, twisting the nights away with the other krauts down at the International Centre. I could just see her, arms akimbo, swivelling hard – up, down, up, down. Nobody could bridge a cultural gap like that. I'd just been kidding myself. The relationship was doomed from the outset, over before it began. I was disappointed. I was angry. Who the hell did she think she was anyway, standing *me* up?

I fumed, cursing her, cursing krauts.

What was I doing messing with krauts? Me, who'd practically been raised on *Reach for the Sky* and *The Dam Busters*. I bet I could still hum the tune, recite snatches of dialogue.

'It's Nigger, sir. He's dead.'

Poor old Nigger. He didn't stand much of a chance. And all of us knew who was to blame. Now I was planning to bring one of them over for coffee and jazz.

'Ve hev fun, ja?'

What kind of language was that?

A harsh language, ugly and cruel. It would take more than a nudge in the right direction. More than a kick and a shove. But I didn't have time. I'd given her a golden opportunity, it wasn't my fault if she'd failed to grasp it. Perhaps she didn't realise who she was dealing with. I wasn't just anybody. I was Ned Selby, King of the Road. And she was just plain Martha. Martha from Müchen. Well, Martha, it was good while it lasted. But nothing is permanent, all things must pass.

'Ve hev fun, ja?'

The words rang in my ears, bringing a pang of regret. She hadn't been so bad really. A little stocky, perhaps, ruddy of cheek, somewhat lacking in inner self. But she wasn't evil. Not all of these Germans were. Still, none of that mattered now. It was over.

Then I thought, maybe it wasn't.

I went back to her words.

'Ve go dancing, ja?'

'Sex is normal, ja?'

Were these the words of a fickle, capricious woman? No, of course, they weren't. I'd been a fool, a pessimistic fool. She was bound to turn up.

I jumped out of bed, laughing now, babbling in tongues.

'Ich bin ein Berliner,' I cried.

Suddenly, I remembered all her funny little foreign ways, her healthy appetite, the way her face lit up when she spoke of the sea and the peppermint twist. I began whispering her name, repeating it over and over. It wasn't a bad name. Not tricksy like Agate, but not plain either. It was wholesome, straightforward and honest. Just like her. Just like the Germans. Sure, there had been one bad apple but you couldn't go on blaming a whole nation. What were boundaries and wars anyway if not the creations of impotent old men who'd forgotten what it was like to be young and in love? This was a new day, a glorious day, and I was ready to forgive and forget.

I went to my window and gazed out over the Selby estate, all quarter of an acre of it. The Minister was mowing the lawn. Backwards and forwards he went, in parallel lines, the nap of the grass more perfect than a bowling green. Ten years of devoted attention – years of sowing and cutting, rolling and dressing – had transformed a patch of barren earth into this lush green sward. It was magnificent. No effort had been thwarted here, this was his canvas, his proper masterpiece, obeying the deep imperatives of his inner self. How poignant it suddenly was to see him with his trousers rolled, damp grass spraying the flannel at his legs. It made me want to do something, I didn't know what. It was a strange, uncomfortable feeling, one I barely recognised, yet one that seemed to stretch a long way back.

Oh mein papa. I forgive you, if you forgive me!

The words just popped into my head. Crazy words, words I didn't understand. I stood there watching him, for a minute or two compelled to watch him. I could see the muscles on his arms stand out as he strained at the mower, his body hunched over it, and as he turned and came back towards the house, an expression on his face I'd never before noticed, relaxed, carefree. He was . . . I didn't know what . . . connected. Happy was an easier word. Christ, I'd never thought of him as being anything before. Not happy, not

70

sad, but simply there, like some huge monument I was forever bumping into, solid, unavoidable, related to me only as an obstacle. His hair had thinned away on top, and he was skinny. That too I'd never noticed. I knew as little of him as he knew of me. Could that be true? I knew he valued learning, chased it in his own haphazard manner. I knew too that education – all those fucking spires – had shut him out, and that he yet retained an awe of it. My two O levels were there between us. Or maybe the other eight that weren't. Plus fat boys, jazz and Susie. In spite of myself I went on looking out. Then suddenly I had a weird and frightening presentiment. For one split second, so brief a moment I almost missed it, I thought – no, I *knew* that he would die at that machine. For an instant I felt the shudder pass through my system, then it was gone, shrugged off.

Death, end, I knew nothing of these things. Nor did I want to. It was Saturday, for Christ's sake. A glorious day, fresh, lucid, wonderful. Martha from München day. Just now she'd be getting up, blonde and lovely, her breath sweet even after sleep. Already I could feel that breath upon my cheeks. I could see her in front of a mirror brushing out her hair, a hundred strokes, to make it shine. One shoulder of her nightdress had slipped down over her left breast and I could see a nipple miraculously erect – yes, like a box of sandwiches. Then I saw her bathe. Or was it shower. These Continentals liked to shower, I knew. It would be one of those little differences we'd discuss, the pros and cons of each, laughing as we did so, in our own private lovers' code. Then she was choosing an outfit, hesitating over something orange. No, Martha, I called. Not orange. Make it black. Plenty of black. Yes, *and* underneath. Oh, take my breath away, surprise me.

I turned from the window excited, expectant, anxious. I

rushed to wash and dress. New scants, old shoes. A splash of after-shave on the tops of my thighs. Perhaps I was falling in love.

I arrived at the El Sol bang on twelve o'clock. I found Martha downstairs, engrossed in a bowl of paella. She was wearing an orange trouser suit, but it wasn't just that which upset me. She was sitting at our table, Susie's and mine. What flagrant presumption! What fucking nerve! Why, she was to Susie as a prune to a peach. Instantly everything seeped from my mood, hopes, dreams, everything. Grains of rice soiled the precious formica. I wanted to sweep them away, to sweep Martha away. How dare she sit there? In orange, munching paella. Hadn't I said black? I was sure I'd said black.

I felt only rage.

'Guten Tag,' Martha said when she saw me.

You Hun! You Vandal! Don't start something with me.

'You vant some paella?' she asked, waving a spoon in my face.

The room lurched. I swayed, clutching my head.

'You are sick, ja?'

'Ja,' I muttered. 'Awfully sick. Back in a minute.'

I rushed upstairs to the loo. Sitting, I managed to calm myself down. What the hell was the matter? Susie was long gone, engaged to a farmer. I must have been crazy. I splashed water on my face, waiting. Then I went back.

I sat down, drawing deep breaths.

'That's better,' I told her. 'It always hits me in basements. Nothing to worry about. I got locked in a cupboard when I was a kid. Haven't got over it yet. Forget it. I try to. Anyway, tell me how you are.'

'Hungry,' she said.

I was certain she'd said angry.

'Angry? Didn't I just explain. I got locked in . . . '

'Nein,' she said. '*Hun*gry.'

I looked at the bowl of fast-disappearing food, then at her jaws working.

'Well,' I said shortly. 'You should be all right in a minute.'

She nodded, swallowing hard.

'Zis feesh,' she exclaimed. 'Is gut, ja?'

We were off and running. The crisis had passed.

'Ja,' I mimicked. 'Is gut.'

She leant forward, tapping her cheek. I examined it carefully, wondering what I might find. A little rouge. Pores that could swallow you whole. Not much else. Perhaps a bit of a tan. But no spot or blemish. She tapped it again, this time pursing her lips.

Of course! Another thing Continentals loved to do. I nipped at the spot. Two smells mingled, struggling against each other for precedence. Soap and feesh. I knew which one I wanted to come out ahead. She turned the other cheek. I pecked that one too.

Then there was an awkward lull in the proceedings. Martha finished her food and sat back, sighing with satisfaction. But I was in trouble again, this time hopelessly lost for words. Do you like dogs? Children? None of them seemed right. I sat there groping, utterly ashamed of myself. Tiny rivers of sweat started to spring at my armpits.

'So . . . ' I began. Then died.

Oh Christ, I thought, let's cut this. It's impossible. I can't stand fish. I hate the colour orange. I'm not even sure I like krauts. I want to play golf. Yes, I'm sorry. A prior arrangement. I know, very rude. But it's my parents, you see . . .

Desperately, I broke into German.

'You hev been busy, ja?'

'Ja,' she replied enthusiastically. 'I find ze International Centre. Is gut, but I speak too much German.' She laughed, then turned her face for another examination.

'You see ze tan. I go zwimming. You know St Paul's pool?'

I knew it all right, but I hadn't been there since I was ten or eleven. One summer I'd slipped, fully clothed, off a grass verge and had had to be rescued from the deep end. The place was crowded and thousands had laughed.

'Yes,' I said. I hung my head forlornly. 'But I don't swim.'

'Ze cupboard?' she asked sympathetically.

I nodded.

'Is a pity,' she said.

'Oh, I don't know,' I said. 'I think my time in the cupboard gave me my artistic bent.'

'Ah,' she exclaimed. 'Ze poetry. Ze dreams.'

Now I was getting it, improvising freely. I decided I'd chance it.

'Last night I had a dream about you,' I said.

'Ja,' she cried eagerly.

'I was also in it.'

I paused tantalisingly.

'Tell me,' she urged.

I leant forward, lowering my voice.

'We were in a room, a white room. We were naked.'

I stopped to check that she'd followed my drift. Her eyes were wide, her lips slightly apart. I took these as good signs. Then I rattled on quickly.

'We were holding hands in front of a window which overlooked a perfect lawn.'

'Vat is lawn?'

'Grass. Like the Backs. The backs of the colleges.'

74

She nodded.

'Anyway, a man was cutting it. A thin man. He was going backwards and forwards along its length. As he did so the grass got greener and greener. Finally when it was almost luminous, the man turned, looked up at us, smiled and waved. He said something, then he disappeared completely. Just melted into the air.'

'Vat did he say? Vat did he say?'

'He said: "The grass is always greener".'

She frowned, mulling it over.

'Vat does it mean?'

I raised my arms, an enigmatic gesture, philosophical.

'On the other side,' I explained, 'the grass is *always* greener.'

A minor triumph. I sat back, pleased as punch.

'Ach,' she said. 'You zink too much.'

Then she poked me, hard in the ribs.

I peeked at my watch below the table-top. Half an hour had passed. My, how time flew by when you were having fun. Still, I needed to speed everything up. I'd reckoned on a safe five hours before the golfers returned, but I hadn't allowed for this sparkling conversation. It was time to risk everything.

'Shall we go?' I said, finishing my drink.

'Ver?' she asked.

'Out to my place.'

She hesitated for a second, then said, 'Is it far?'

I indicated that it was some distance from the town centre.

'You hev a car?'

I shook my head. Then I had another bright idea.

'No, but I've got a Vespa.'

'Vat is Vespa?' she asked.

75

'A scooter. You know, Italian. Mine's light blue, a good little runner.'

Her face brightened.

'Gut,' she said, slapping the table. 'Ve hev fun, ja!'

'We certainly will,' I said. 'But I don't actually have it this minute. I lent it to a friend. We can catch a bus, though, close by, no trouble at all.'

At the other end I gave Martha the scenic route, through the women's college. And that was almost a mistake. For a minute I didn't think we'd get past the pond. She was on her back in a trice, gurgling about swimming and tans. I scrambled for an excuse to get on – hay fever, heat bumps, bad eyes – but luckily I remembered the cupboard. I was already emotionally unsound; it wouldn't do to pile on anything else. These Germans were hardly renowned for their compassion towards the unfortunate. I was gloomily resigning myself to the loss of another hour when she looked up and apologised. I think it had something to do with my childhood trauma. I thanked her for the indulgence, but said it was quite all right, apart from the heat bumps I was fine in the sun.

We walked on along the shaded, wooded path. She took off her jacket. Underneath she had on a fluffy white V-necked sweater. With my eyes I searched in vain for an erect nipple. She was wearing some fiendish piece of engineering, all wires and uplift. I could see the ribbed outlines of the material, and her breasts stood out, firm and immobile. My vision blurred. All I could see was fluffy white. And tits. Big tits. I took her hand. A little squeeze, a smile. Five yards further on I pulled her to me. I felt the twin encasement at my chest. Should I grope now or later? Her tongue found mine, duelled, withdrew. I could smell paella, a faint whiff of shrimp. Despite this my dander was very definitely up,

76

uncomfortably hooked into the folds of my scants. I daren't look down. It was huge, embarrassingly vast. Suddenly, we were emerging from the trees, back on the street. My street. My parents' street. I saw net curtains move, fingers pointing. Then I heard whispers.

'Look, look! The dirty beast. Could have been another Arnold Palmer. Now he's bringing a Nazi home. What will his mother say when I tell her?'

NO, PLEASE. NOT THAT!

I must have shouted out loud, for Martha said:

'Vat?'

Then I said, 'What?'

Then she said, 'You said, please!'

Then I said, 'I'm sorry, I was thinking.'

'Ach,' she said. 'You zink too much.'

I smiled wanly.

Yes, I thought. I zink too much.

I whisked Martha as quickly as I could through the ground floor of the house up to my room. Even so, she noticed the worn stair carpets, the home-made lamp standards. Once she was inside and I'd closed the door, she said:

'Zey must be very poor, ja, your landlord and landlady?'

My heart sank. The whole thing was a mistake, a wretched mistake. Did it have to be like this? Surely sometimes it was painless, easy? I busied myself with my Belling, hiding my face.

'They don't have a lot of money,' I said. 'They have a son. They send him to school.'

'Ah,' she said. 'Zey make sacrifices.'

Jesus, I thought.

'Zey take in lodgers.'

I spooned out the coffee.

'He is lucky, no?'

77

I was almost in tears. Any more of this and I'd be sobbing like a baby.

'I know he's grateful,' I said in a faltering voice.

Martha moved to the window. As she did so she stumbled over one of the yellow snakeskins. She shrieked, jumping aside in alarm, 'Vat is zat?'

I kicked it out of the way, under the bed with its pair.

'A shoe,' I said. 'Snakeskin, yellow, very long, very narrow.'

'Ach,' she snorted. 'Vat kind of people vear shoes like zat?'

I let that one pass.

She looked out over the lawn, then turned back suddenly with a knowing grin on her face, the kind of grin which in her case was usually accompanied by a solid poke in the ribs.

'Ze dream, ja?' She walked towards me. Then it came. Good natured, but solid. 'Ve vere naked, ja?'

I was still making the coffee, but managed a smile as I toppled back on to my arse.

Then she was at my records, flicking through the pile. I watched her face for signs of recognition. Nothing. I saw my favourites go by. Errol, Miles, the MJQ. She didn't even pause to say hi. Half-way through she lost interest.

'All zeze black men, but no Chubby Checker,' she said. 'Nozzing to dance to.'

'Now that's where you're wrong,' I said keenly.

I got up, elbowed her out of the way, and found an old Blue Note album, 'The Sounds of Jimmy Smith'. Just a hammond organ, drums and guitar. I slapped it on the turntable, selecting a twelve-minute version of 'Blue Moon' with an extended, rippling guitar solo by Eddie McFadden. I'd danced to it a hundred times. Anyone could dance to it.

But not her. For thirty seconds she swivelled, beating the air with her arms, then abruptly gave up.

'Ver is ze zinging?' she asked.

'It's an instrumental,' I snapped. Eddie was just beginning his solo, myriad notes cascading from the opening melodic line, a brilliant pyrotechnic display.

'You listen to *this*,' I demanded.

I closed my eyes, and let the notes spill over me, grunting appreciatively in all the right places.

'Well?' I asked when it was over.

'Vel, vat?' she replied.

'What did you think?'

'I didn't hear zo gut,' she said. 'You make too many noises.'

Ach, I thought disgustedly.

How wonderful it was to be young and in love and getting my kicks.

I poured out the coffee. She took hers and sat on the bed, propping herself up on the pillows, sipping slowly. I sat opposite, on the floor with my back to the wall. Her thighs bulged beneath her orange trousers. I glanced at them surreptitiously, then at the fluffy white sweater. Something stirred in my scants, I was no longer sure what. All of a sudden I had a vision of what we able-bodied beats did at times like this, after coffee and jazz. It was a vision from which I was oddly separate, but there we both were. I sipped, she sipped. She bulged, I watched. Then I got up. I wavered a second, then plopped down beside her. I felt wooden, and unreal, driven now by a sense of what I ought to be doing, not by any inkling of what I wanted to do.

Seduction by numbers started at once. Reach out hand, two three. Pause, two three. Smile, two three. I grappled with acres of white, then at the barriers below.

'Nein,' she cried sharply. 'Nein.'

My whole body stiffened, flooding with fear. Headlines flashed in my mind — ex-public-schoolboy charged with assault. Parents blame coffee and jazz. Innocent girl's four-hour ordeal. I was about to start begging when she stood up and whipped off her sweater.

'Thank God,' I gasped in relief.

I don't think she'd ever had a reaction like that, for she jumped up and down with delight. Suddenly I wanted to go home. Then I remembered I *was* home. I was locked in a cupboard, and thousands were laughing.

'Ve hev fun, ja,' she cried.

I nodded weakly. I felt my head fall off and roll some distance away. I watched it go, gently rocking to stillness in a corner of the room.

'Are you all right?' I heard across space. The words took two or three minutes to reach me.

'Fine,' I spat. 'Why not? Don't I look it?'

'Perhaps ze cupboard . . . ' she began.

'No,' I broke in. 'Nothing the matter.'

She stood there in her panties and bra. I could hardly believe it. The bra was white, wired for extra support. A thing like that could poke your eyes out. Her panties were pale green, a sort of aertex, large and sensible. Not a trace of black anywhere.

'I am ready, ja,' she said.

She sat on the bed, beckoning.

Right, I thought, there's a time to live and a time to die. I tore off my shirt. Then I struggled out of my jeans, lurching wildly around the room on one leg. Martha lay back giggling.

'Whatsamatter?' I stammered.

'Ze peppermint twist,' she said, pointing as I bounced off a wall.

That did it. I dived half the width of the room, flopping beside her. I rolled on to her body, frenziedly tearing at fabric and mounds of flesh.

'Nein,' Martha called again, slapping my hand. I flipped off quickly. Then she was arching her back. A strap sprang and her breasts burst free. I gaped at them, awed, a gurgling sound in my throat. Suddenly I was nuzzling hard. I couldn't help myself. I slurped, I drooled, I gurgled. I was overwhelmed. It was too much, too soon. Any moment I was certain to come. I tried thinking of my mother. I counted fat boys. I bit my lip. None of it made any difference. Beep, beep. There it was. I fell away totally shamed, hiding my soiled scants, humiliated by my own member. Martha wiped off her thighs.

'Your first time, ja? It can happen ze first time.'

'No,' I blurted. 'Hundreds of times. Don't know what went wrong. It won't happen again. I promise.'

She reached out and patted me, a kindly expression on her face.

'For how long ver you locked in zat cupboard?' she asked.

I hated her then. She was laughing at me, joining in with all the other bathers.

'Ve vill vait,' she said confidently.

I wanted to be alone with my hurt pride and sticky scants, but I was trapped in my own room, all exits barred by a near-naked German. Wait for what? After what happened we might be waiting all day. And the next. First time, indeed. I still remembered the first time. It wasn't like this. It was with Susie. In a meadow, down by the river. The sun

81

was shining. I felt good afterwards.

I turned towards Martha. Her eyes were closed, and one arm lay languidly behind her head on the pillow. Then I gazed at her tits. Nothing languid about those, they were twinned lambs that would frisk in the sun. For some reason I could see her on a beach clutching a large ball, everything bouncing. A nude beach crowded with laughing Germans, all of them casually naked.

From a long way off I felt stirrings again, coming gradually closer. I strained to help them on their way. Martha woke up with a grunt. I knew if she stopped me now I'd never recover. I strained. I prayed. Lord have mercy. Then she drew off her panties. Bravely, I slid down to the dark, thrusting my face between her legs. First time! I'd give her first time. I lapped and sucked, lapped and sucked. I could barely breathe. Like a swimmer I had to keep coming up for air. A breath every third stroke, then under again. I worked for five minutes, then I felt a hand in my hair, pulling my head up.

'Not zere,' a voice hissed. '*Zere!*'

Frantically I did as I was bid, lapping and slurping. Then I touched something and Martha twitched. I did it again. She gasped. I went into overdrive, right on the spot. Martha writhed and moaned and twitched. I couldn't believe my skill. I was a real talent, a genius! Suddenly there was a great yelp, and Martha went into a prolonged spasm.

'Jawohl!,' she bellowed. 'Jawohl!'

I slipped to the floor, panting, grinning triumphantly. Then I got up and strode to my wardrobe. I was on top of it now, a bloody hero, king of the beats. I found the package amongst my socks, I took off my scants, tore open the foil, and rolled on with a practised ease. First time! What a fucking joke! Then I swaggered back to the bed.

82

Martha was sitting up, resting on her elbows. She looked grand. I felt grand. Everything was grand. I lay down, murmuring her name. Martha, from München. The 'th' hard. I sidled across her body, lowering myself gently onto her belly. I groped down there, finding my way. She helped. I was grateful. This was how it should be. Effortless, easy, two bodies merging, flowing into each other. It was warm. It was wonderful. It was home.

HOME!

The word went off like a bomb, the first in a cluster. MOTHER. FATHER. ON THEIR WAY NOW. SHAME. FAT BOYS. INSANITY. DEATH.

I sprang up, everything limp, slipping. Aghast, Martha cowered back in the pillows.

'*Was? Was?*' she shouted, her voice almost a screech.

I slapped my forehead, trying to think. Then I stumbled aimlessly about picking up clothes. Scants, socks, bra, panties.

'Was? Was?' she shouted again.

I caught glimpses of Martha's face, hideously distorted. Then she spat out a stream of German.

'Warum? Warum? . . . Ich habe die nase voll!'

A harsh language, ugly and cruel.

'Dress, please!' I begged.

I tossed her her bra.

'I vant a shower,' she said, refusing to move.

'NO SHOWER . . . ONLY A BATH . . . TAKES FAR TOO LONG . . . QUICK.'

I pulled everything on. Martha watched. Finally she stood up and began dressing herself.

'Thank you,' I blurted. 'Thank you. You're saving my life. Do let me help.'

I rushed towards her, flailing my arms.

'Was is das?' she cried, shoving me away. 'You are med, ja?'

I slumped on the bed. I owed it to her to come clean. She was a nice girl, kind and considerate.

'I lied,' I explained. 'But I did it for love. I live with my parents. They'll be home in a minute.'

She just stared at me, shaking her head. Then she started. 'Schweinhund,' she said softly. 'You hev no respect. For zem or for me. Zey sacrifice everyzing.'

She paused, looked around at the room, then said, 'Zese . . . zese are your keeks. You are a child, ja?'

I didn't have the heart to argue. Something in her manner told me it was over. We finished dressing in silence. I offered to walk her to the bus-stop, but she wanted none of it, none of me. I stood at the door and watched her go. Then I went back to my room.

Later, much later, I heard a car turn into our drive.

8

That night I had another bad dream. I was at work, but I'd hidden out in the kitchen to avoid any embarrassing contact with Martha. Half-way through the lunch-time rush Andy poked his head round the swing door.

'Ned,' he told me. 'There's a couple of bruisers out here asking for Selby. I'm pretty certain they're German.'

I'd been half-expecting a visit because I knew Martha had written home. Even so, I went weak at the knees.

'What do they look like?' I asked.

'Short cropped hair,' he said. 'Sabre scars. Plenty of bone below the eyes.'

I nodded helplessly, anticipating the worst.

'What did they order?'

'Paella,' he said.

Now there was no doubt at all.

'Where are they?' I asked.

'Downstairs,' he answered.

'At *my* table?' I groaned.

'Yes,' he said gently. 'Spilling rice all over the formica.'

I groaned again. I could run but I couldn't hide. Perhaps if I gave myself up they'd go easy on me. After all they knew my psychological weaknesses already: heat bumps, cupboards, and worn carpets. If I whimpered and whined maybe they'd leave me alone.

'Andy,' I choked, one hand touching his shoulder. 'If I don't see you again, remember your snakeskin winklepickers. They're under the bed in my room.'

'Fine,' he said. 'How were they?'

'A little tight,' I told him.

I pushed open the door, and staggered towards the stairs.

For almost a week I hid out in the kitchen, waiting. I knew some sort of disaster would strike, even if it wasn't the one in my dream. Perhaps if I worked the machine it would explode in my face, permanently emblazoning shame across my hitherto perfect features. Or maybe Martha would show, bringing with her a bunch of unctuous foreigners from the International Centre to gawp and giggle and insult me in public. Or perhaps the neighbours were already at work, buzzing my mother with snippets of poisonous information.

'Nice round on Saturday, Mrs Selby?'

'Lovely, thank you, but my short game was nothing to speak of. I didn't know you were interested in golf?'

'Oh yes, Mrs Selby. I've always been a big fan of Arnold Palmer's. I hear your Ned used to display some of his talent. Of course, I know that's a few years ago now.'

A flush of remnant pride for my early triumphs would

appear in my mother's face, then disappointment at my present neglect. The neighbour would shake her head, a malign grin spreading across her features.

'Still,' she'd say knowingly. 'I bet he makes more than a few birdies up in that salon of his when you and your husband are out.'

But the machine didn't explode. Nor did Martha show up. As for my mother and neighbours, each night I went home I stopped some distance from the house, checking for drawn blinds, the signal for me to make myself scarce and slink in later when everyone was in bed. But the blinds stayed open all week, and all week my mother's face showed no signs of the strain with which I was so familiar. Her eyes weren't swollen from weeping, her skin was free of livid red blotches. To my great relief these infallible meters of sorrow presently registered zero.

For a time I was a little more attentive to both my parents, a little less sure of my ground. Once or twice I stayed in, watching the TV, sitting with them like in the old days that weren't, in fact, so very old, but for the Minister my presence in that room, on that sofa, seemed to evoke Agate's absence and brought into focus the unresolved battle of wills between us. Soon I was back in my room, with Errol and Brigitte and Jack. But I was quiet and reflective. I didn't play jazz. Brigitte remained on her shelf. Jack just gathered dust. As a beat I was a bit of a failure. Martha had called me a child, and that's just how I felt. I felt trapped, if you like, between her and my folks. But not her as Martha, flesh, blood and bone from München. Rather as what she represented in terms of the limits of my current possibilities. Another interpretation, more appropriate now that I saw it, was that I felt trapped somewhere between *me* and my folks. I could neither abide by their definitions nor define myself. I simply responded. I examined the whole of my life. Pre-school, prep school, upper school. I'd always felt constrained, on hold. Yes, I'd simply reacted. To what, rightly or wrongly, I'd felt was imposed. Who was I? What was I? Not them. Certainly not them. But who? Not Arnold, or Sam. I wasn't Errol. I wasn't Andy. Not Jack. Not even Falmer. I was me. But I wasn't myself. I was a set of responses, negative, angry responses which eventually filled me with guilt and remorse.

What's more, I was alone again. Oh, I put on a brave face. To Andy I lied, the way you do – sure, she was hot stuff . . . No, no trouble with the room . . . Who knows, I might see her again . . . A casual arrangement – giving him a line commensurate with my status in the hierarchy of beatdom, but the truth was I felt lonely and thwarted. Thwarted! I never thought I'd share anything with the old fellow. Was this how he felt? Sick, empty, insignificant?

I got up. I went to work. I came home. I went to bed. Life! A dismal round of disappointments. I saw girls everywhere, beautiful, tall, intelligent, kind. But they weren't for me. They were older, sure of themselves, linked with captains of industry and scholars. I fell in love secretly, hopelessly: Anita, the ravishing brunette I glimpsed on a bridge by the river, swathed in cotton and lace, her mouth enticingly crooked, her green eyes flashing; Delia, the dark-skinned window-dresser who moved so beautifully behind the glass. Ah, the times I paced backwards and forwards watching her change the displays. Impossible, frightening. There were many. And there were none. I was outside looking in. I was neither this nor that. Not one thing or the other.

I spent too much time thinking, getting tangled in a web of impossible conundrums. Finally I just responded. I got angry again. I was alone, but whose fault was that? Not mine. Certainly not mine. I had everything: a room with a view, records, two books. I was man enough for any woman. The world was to blame. The world of parents and golf, conventions and Germans. I knew what to expect if I scorned the world. Rejection from all sides. They'd never understand, not in a million years. It would be this way always. The only question was did I have the guts for the struggle. Better men than I had gone under. Van Gogh, for example. Hadn't he sliced off an ear? It was probably red and slightly translucent. It hadn't made any difference. One ear or two, he was still ignored by the crowd. He was a man alone. I was a man alone. Me. Ned Selby.

9

One night soon after I'd recuperated I went over to Andy's. He was having a soirée, he said. That's what he called it. He rolled his eyes at the word, letting it stand out, with a suggestion that it would be worth my while if I put in an appearance. I rang his bell about eight. After a minute his mother answered the door, inviting me in immediately. Some mother! She was still groomed, elegant. Still smiling. She had on a pleated skirt which swung loosely just below the knees, and a bright Paisley blouse. For an instant I fell in love with her, but that way madness lay, so I fell quickly out again.

'Come in, Ned,' she said. 'Andy's upstairs. You know the way.'

I shuffled in, then caught myself manically wiping my feet on the mat.

'Thank you, Mrs Stuart,' I said.

Another smile. Perfect teeth flashing.

'Call me Judith. Everyone else does.'

She said it easily, no hint of pretension. But at that moment it seemed even more difficult than calling my mother Mary. I made it to the stairs, turned, and smiled disconcertedly back. Mrs Stuart – Judith – had already disappeared. I carried on up. At the top of the stairs I heard music coming from beyond Andy's door, big-band music, with a delicate female voice up front. I paused for a moment, listening. I thought I recognised the piano, Teddy Wilson, but from an entirely different setting. The Benny Goodman trio, Goodman himself, Gene Krupa and Wilson. This was an orchestra, and I'd never heard the singer before. I stood outside for a little while longer, then I knocked.

'Hi, man,' Andy said. 'I didn't hear the bell. Did Judith let you in?'

Judith again. I nodded. One thing was certain: Andy would never have to slice off an ear.

'Hi,' I said, dropping 'man' for the present.

I stepped inside. The girl spoke first.

'Hi, man,' she said.

Her voice was plummy, top-notch. I thought I knew it from somewhere.

'Ned, this is Julie,' said Andy.

I stretched out a hand, then when it wasn't taken, waved. She was sitting in a chair, legs drawn up under her. She wore black eye-shadow and mauve nail varnish. She had on jeans and a battered navy-blue rollneck sweater. A scarf over her hair matched the colour of the varnish. It was that which placed her. She was the girl from the alley, the one who was in with the band. One of the select few who didn't have to pay for a ticket. I felt I needed to make an instant impression.

91

'Teddy Wilson,' I said. 'But who's the singer?'

She looked at me as if I was less than shit, then threw a glance at Andy.

'Jesus,' she said. '*You* tell him.'

Immediately, I felt thwarted.

'Billie Holiday,' he said.

'Lady Day,' she added. The way she said it implied they were intimates. Well, maybe they were. I had the same relationship with Errol but I wasn't exclusive about it. I sat down. It was obvious I was going to have to listen, for no more concessions were made to my entrance. At first I resented being made to feel like an intruder, but almost at once I was in thrall to the haunting melancholy of that voice. Songs I thought were just corny old ballads – 'I'll Get By', 'On the Sentimental Side', 'If Dreams Came True' – were transformed by the singer's treatment of them into the most aching elegies of despair. Tempo made no difference, nor did the pre-bebop formality of the arrangements. The voice was everything, sounding depths of sorrow and pain and loss I couldn't even begin to estimate. For me, something about the whole experience was like being in church, the way I remembered it years before at Christmas and Easter, when the Minister would drag me out, and I'd go unwillingly, never sure why, but still be touched by the solemnity of the architecture, or the ritual, or I didn't know what. I was awed before it, feeling, however inchoately, the frightful proximity of unhappiness, of tragedy. Holiday's voice did that to me then. And suddenly after all those songs, so voluptuous in their sorrow, IT, that tragedy, came. A voice, barely recognisable, cracked and broken. 'For all we know, we may never meet again.' It shook me rigid.

In the silence afterwards, I heard myself say, 'Christ, what happened?'

'Life happened,' Julie said. 'She got screwed is what happened. By her father, by the police, by everyone.'

There was still that edge in Julie's conversation, aggressive, perhaps bitter, but it was no longer directed at me. Still, I was unnerved. Also intrigued. Here was a woman who had no concern with the likes of Chubby Checker. She gave me a brief resumé of Holiday's life, then Andy flipped the record over and we listened to the other side. My attention swung between the new songs and speculations, or at any rate questions, about Julie. Where did she come from? What did she do? The most amazing thing to me was that she really did know the music. Every so often she'd grin with anticipated delight, raise a finger to attract our notice, then lead us, or perhaps just me, through a particularly subtle phrase or variation. I couldn't help grinning too, at least afterwards, for her accuracy was unerring. To begin with she checked my reactions, or maybe I just thought she did, as if I was undergoing some sort of test which I had to pass if I was to win a portion of her approval. But then that stopped, and then when we looked each other's way it seemed to me that it was simply to share the same current of understanding and pleasure.

The side finished and Julie got up to switch records. When she went back to her chair she gave Andy a meaningful look. Some current of understanding, or careful consideration, must have passed between them, for Andy said suddenly, 'Of course. Why not?'

Then she was dipping into the bag at her side, drawing out a loose newspaper package. This she placed on her knees, then went back to her bag to pull out cigarettes and hand-rolling papers. I thought that was a bit weird. Why on earth would she want both? And I felt a sense of untoward drama in the procedure so I went on observing closely. Julie

93

stuck three papers together in a curious manner making a large rectangle with one gummed edge still free, and I thought, well, OK, so she likes a big cigarette, expecting her to dip back into her bag for a two-ounce tin of Old Holborn. Not a bit of it. She reached out for a record sleeve, put that on her knees, pulled a factory-made cigarette from its box, promptly broke it apart, then sprinkled the tobacco evenly along the middle of the paper rectangle. I glanced at Andy. No explanation, he just grinned, engrossed in the spectacle. I turned back to Julie. Now she was carefully unfolding the newspaper package, as though it might suddenly go off in her hands. She peeled back the edges, flattening them, then stopped. She looked up, an expression of pride on her face. At the centre of the rumpled newspaper was what appeared to be a small mound of pressed leaves, dried, green and brittle.

'Good,' she said. 'Only a few seeds.'

I was about to say something daft concerning lawns and the Minister when the great wave suddenly hit me. My God, there it was! Reefer, weed, marijuana, grass! Who'd have believed it? For a moment or two, I almost didn't. I just stared at the stuff. I'd never seen it before, I didn't even know much about it. A couple of scenes from *On the Road* sprang immediately to mind, but beyond that all I knew was that Gene Krupa had done time in the forties for possession. Krupa, with his wild grin and elaborate showmanship, was an old hero of mine. He always looked like a man having fun. Maybe it was that. The stuff looked harmless enough, and the words reefer and grass certainly had a comfortable, reassuring sound. But there was another word, a dead word, redolent of needles and jail, and of the hoarse and collapsed voice I'd heard a few minutes before. DRUG. A confusion of images, words and feelings welled up. Reefer, drug. Drug, reefer. Fat boys. O levels. Sacrifice. Jazz. Fun. Kicks. Head-masters. Lawns. Golf. I was enticed and deterred in about equal measure. My heart pounded. I could hear it. They could hear it. But no, Julie just rolled, concerned only with spillage. Two or three minutes later she produced a tight cylinder, narrow at one end, broad at the other. Into the narrow she pushed a cardboard filter, then placed the whole thing in her mouth, twisted it around her lips, withdrew it, then finally held it up for inspection. Andy murmured his cheerful approval, but I still wasn't clear what I was looking at, what it all meant. Julie sensed my caution.

'First time?' she said.

Hadn't I heard that before, just recently? On this occasion there was no denying it.

'Don't worry,' she said. 'It'll make you feel good. You won't be an addict or anything. This is just grass.'

Just grass.

Of course!

Drug was a word from the world of convention and Germans, parents and golf. I knew what to expect from that world. Dumb words and misinformation.

Julie lit up and drew hard on the cylinder. I noticed that she held on to the smoke and that when she exhaled hardly any came out. That was important, she said. She drew several lungfuls, deftly dampening down a fast-burning side with saliva, then she passed it to Andy. It wasn't his first time. He took three big confident pulls, making short suc-king noises with his mouth, then he breathed out and handed it over to me. I grasped it between my fingers. It spluttered there, a squib on a short fuse. Light blue touch paper and stand clear. I looked at Andy, Julie, then, with a sigh only I heard, I raised it to my lips.

I had three hits. Nothing. I rasped a little. I looked at the

others. The cigarette did the rounds again. Three more hits.
I watched, waited, listened.

This is good stuff.

It certainly is.

Fresh from Tangiers. Ever been there?

Why, no.

You really should.

I always meant to.

Has everything . . . mint tea . . . Arabs . . . fields of grass
. . . uncle Bill . . .

Who?

Burroughs. Uncle Bill Burroughs.

I thought he was invisible.

He doesn't get out much, it's true.

No?

Just stares at his feet all day.

His feet!

Yes.

Well, you've got to do something.

How about some music?

What would you like?

Then all of a sudden I could feel it. That moment. The one
in which everything is about to arrive and you know everything for ever. I couldn't help myself. Out of some wild blue
yonder I put on a German accent and barked:

'Chubby Checker.'

Then I laughed. And howled. And stamped my feet.
Christ, I was a fucking fire-eater. Me. Ned Selby. One of the
select few. Puffing a reefer. I rocked in my seat, gasping for
breath.

'There he goes . . . just look at him . . . a dope fiend . . .
you can tell by the walk . . . the rhythm . . . the swagger.
First it was sex, darky music, now it's the drugs. I've lived

here nigh on twenty years and I've never seen anything like it.'

Andy and Julie were laughing now. With me, or at me, I didn't care which. I simply got that they'd got that I'd got it. It was absurd, crazy. I laughed. They laughed. A great deluge of laughter, swamping us all. What coffee we drank! What biscuits we ate! What music we heard! I was elated by a powerful new sense of communion. Ned Selby, this is your life. Unique, bold, destined for wonderful things.

It seemed like only a minute but five hours had zipped by. I sat there trying to get up. I looked at my legs. Reluctant, disobedient legs, the legs of a dope fiend. Come on legs.

Finally, they stirred. One step, two steps. I was getting the hang of it.

'Andy, Julie,' I said. 'I'm going outside now. I might be gone for some time.'

Fortunately, I didn't run into Judith on the stairs. I walked home in the dark, singing 'If dreams came true'.

10

The face. An outward expression of the inner self. As with one, so with the other. Both were beginning to change. Hair a little longer, stubble more pronounced. And the eyes, suffused with the light of a new understanding, a new knowledge.

Ah, the miracle of grass. All at once everything was cool. Andy was cool. Julie was cool. Even the Minister and Mary were cool. They didn't know it, but they were. I was flesh of their flesh, blood of their blood. I wanted to share my new knowledge with them, to share the fruits of their sacrifice. But they came from a different time, a different place. They'd never understand, not in a million years. Look what their world had done to Gene. A man who laughed, a man who played jazz. In the eyes of their world the eyes of a dope fiend stared back at me from the mirror.

I was a criminal!

How stupid. How utterly, unbelievably stupid.

It was a joke. A sick joke.

From my station on the machine I began to examine the faces of the public. Did I see happiness, pleasure? Balls! All I could find was a general malaise. I wanted to reach out, to shout. Seek and ye shall find! Ask and it shall be given! Try this, it'll make you feel good, you won't be an addict or anything.

But I had to keep my knowledge to myself. I was a criminal, forced by prejudice and ignorance into a twilight world of secret rooms and hazardous trysts.

Ah, but it was fun too. For they, the squares, were many; and we, the beats, were few. Us and them, a lovely distinction. I sloped along, smiling indulgently at the poor unfortunates, puff, puff, infinitely tolerant, a superior man with the truth in his pocket.

I spent most of my time with Andy and Julie now, either at her place or his. What with my near miss with Martha I'd left off entertaining at home. Besides, Julie rented a large room above a Chinese restaurant quite near the El Sol and it was easy and convenient to go there with Andy after work. Two weeks after my initiation soirée I was visiting, getting whacked as usual, when Andy made the announcement.

'We're going to Paris,' he said.

I took a hit of the reefer, big and confident now, then said flippantly,

'Good. You need a holiday from that till. In fact that till needs a holiday from you.'

'Not a holiday,' he said grinning. 'We're moving. At least for a while.'

It seemed an incomprehensible notion to me. Despite my gift for languages, I'd never been anywhere except Cromer and Devon. But Paris, well, that was abroad. A place where they did funny things with salads.

'What for?' I asked.

It was a foolish question, and I cringed the moment it was out of my mouth. For kicks, of course. What other reason was there for doing anything. Reason was tantamount to purpose. A square word for square people. You lived, you died. No reason, no purpose.

Julie shrugged.

'Why does anyone go to Paris?'

To climb the Eiffel Tower? To gaze at the Mona Lisa? Maybe to catch a glimpse of Brigitte Bardot? I had no idea.

'To *be*,' she said.

I nodded, carefully assessing the import of these two words. Yes, I thought I understood. We were back to kicks, and living for today. On the wall behind Julie's shoulder was a large painting, one of her own. She called it 'Birth'. A big orange eye appeared to be bursting out of an open vagina. She saw me looking at it, and smiled.

'Yes,' she said. '*That's* why.'

I let sudden understanding race into my face. But all I could see was an orange eye and an open vagina.

'The emerging creative principle,' she said. 'Art.'

Of course! Why hadn't I seen it? Birth. The eye. Art. It was blindingly obvious. But Paris? What about Paris?

'Artists and writers have always been drawn to Paris,' she said.

I seemed to remember there was a famous opera with this as a theme. I must have heard it at one of Agate's family's musical evenings, something about a garret, TB, and a beautiful woman called Mimi. But maybe I was muddled.

100

Perhaps it was just a film starring Gene Kelly. Anyway, taking turns, Andy and Julie reeled off a list of names, all expatriate writers and painters: Hemingway, Joyce, Picasso, Fitzgerald, Miller, Ginsberg, Jack. I got the impression that a whole area of Paris known as the Left Bank fairly buzzed with the sound of the emerging creative principle. There was jazz, too. Chet Baker was there. Bud Powell and Johnny Griffiths. Andy and Julie would rub shoulders with these greats, drink wine, smoke dope, and live in the Beat hotel. In such a rarefied atmosphere Andy couldn't fail to achieve the dizzy imaginative heights of his first surrealist masterpiece, the nipple poem. Nor would Julie's eye fail to record such an ebullient scene. Art, freedom. Why, Paris was synonymous with both. You only had to think of those songs. 'April in Paris', 'Under the Bridges', 'Zank 'Eaven for Leetle Girls' . . . .

All of a sudden I felt a pang of envy, but to begin with I wasn't really sure why. For me, leaving was a completely abstract concept. Christ, I'd never even thought there was a place to leave, let alone one to go to. This town was where I lived, no matter what. I couldn't go gallivanting about. People like me didn't.

But the pang had disturbed all that, triggering awkward questions. Why the hell couldn't I? for example. This was the most awkward for I could find no satisfactory answer. It just depressed me, giving me that fleeting but vaguely familiar doubt that perhaps I wasn't quite as good as I thought I was.

Pretty soon, though, I was high and feeling every bit as good as I thought I was. Ned Selby, criminal and dope fiend, a man with unbridled scorn for the world of the unbeat, could do anything. In his own time, he almost certainly would. For the present it was enough for him to just *be*.

101

Here, there, it didn't matter which. Wherever he was was automatically charged with the brilliance of his vision.

'Christ,' I said suddenly. 'What am I going to do about grass after you've gone?'

'I'll speak to my dealer,' Julie said. 'Maybe I can arrange something.'

'Please,' I said, pressing her eagerly. 'It just wouldn't do, being without.'

The Minister and Mary were still up when I got home, pinned to their places in front of the TV. How bloody inconsiderate of them! I was ravenous for cornflakes and milk, but I didn't think I could manage such an intricate operation with potential witnesses in the next room. I was so high it had been a struggle even to find the right house. They all looked so much alike in the dark, two up, two down semis, with garages attached. Ours was number ten. Between nine and eleven. For five minutes I paced backwards and forwards. Nine, eleven. Nine, eleven. There wasn't a trace of ten.

Then I remembered. Odds and evens were on different sides of the street. It didn't seem logical to me. Why not count down one way, and back the other? Better yet, go by flora and fauna. A lilac bush, perfect lawns. Yes, there it was, nestled between eight and twelve.

I crept in, hoping to get up to my room without being noticed, but I seemed to be wearing a pair of heavy diver's boots and my effort was slow, clumsy and loud. Mary called as I went by, clunking up the stairs. I clunked down again and lurched to the door. Inside two strangers were acting out

102

a scene from a play entitled *The Living Room*. A domestic drama involving worn carpets, home-made lamp standards, and a teenage dope fiend. Enter dope fiend.

First stranger (female): 'What's the matter with your eyes? They're all red. (Pause.) Have you been crying?'

Second stranger (male): 'Drinking more like.'

Dope fiend (in diver's boots, laboriously approaching his interrogators): 'Not drinking. Not crying. I had a ride home on a Vespa. Light blue. A good little runner. The wind makes your eyes water.'

First stranger: 'A Vespa? Light blue? It belongs to that Andy.'

Second stranger: 'I'll give you something that'll make your eyes water if you go on gallivanting about. It's high time you snapped out of it, my lad, coming in at all hours.'

Dope fiend (calmly, attempting to alleviate obvious anxieties): 'Don't worry. Everything's cool. The Vespa is cool. Andy is cool. In fact, he's going to Paris.'

Second stranger: 'Best place for him, if you ask me.'

First stranger: 'What's he going to do there?'

Dope fiend (after a pause): 'He's just . . . just going to be.'

Second stranger: 'Be? What do you mean? Be what?'

Dope fiend (airily): 'Writers and artists have always been drawn to Paris. The Left Bank. Hemingway, Fitzgerald, Jack. I was thinking about going myself . . . '

First stranger gasps, horrified by the idea.

Second stranger (dismissively): 'Ach, you wouldn't last five minutes. You don't even travel well. You always got sick in the car just going to Cromer.'

Dope fiend (protestingly): 'I've got French O level.'

Second stranger: 'A failure in two languages. You wouldn't like the food – garlic, olive oil. You'd be back in a week, gobbling cornflakes for all you were worth.'

Dope fiend: 'I love garlic, olive oil. I got that from Agate.'

Second stranger (wistfully breathing the name): 'Agate. Such a nice girl. You'll never find her like.'

Exit dope fiend, left. Lights fade on the two strangers. In another part of the house the dope fiend undresses, climbs into bed, and falls instantly asleep. In his dreams he wanders the boulevards, searching for Brigitte Bardot.

11

Julie was as good as her word. The following Tuesday I got a message from Andy to go by her place after work. He told me the man would be waiting.

I frowned, wondering what on earth he was on about. 'What man?' I asked.

'You know,' he said. '*The* man.'

I still didn't get it.

He rubbed his thumbs and forefingers together in a rapid and precise piece of mime, then took a hit of an imaginary cigarette.

'Oh, man,' I said, in a flash. 'You don't mean *that* man?'

Andy nodded.

Christ, what could he be like? A gangster? A corrupter of

children? Or someone like me with the courage of his convictions, a man with guts enough for the struggle? My feelings ran riot between excitement and fear. I was stepping into the big league, giving up my amateur status, a soon-to-be-genuine beat with a stash of his own.

I took a long circuitous route to Julie's, several times doubling back on my tracks. It was a three-minute walk from the El Sol, but to be on the safe side I made it an hour. I walked over the river strolling casually, nonchantly pausing to tie up a shoe lace, all the while checking on who was behind me. Then I went back into town, threading my way in and out of the crowded bus queues opposite Woolworth's. A couple of characters spooked me, cops if ever I saw them, but I managed to shake them off before diving headlong into the Chinese restaurant. Even then I waited. But nobody came. Finally I went to the stairs, climbed them, and knocked on Julie's door. I used the special dope fiend knock, two sharp raps, followed by a third after a pause.

It was just as well. The acrid smell of grass flooding out into the hallway when Julie opened the door was almost overpowering. She must have been at it for hours. I hurried inside. The shades over the window were pulled to and it took a minute or two for my eyes to adjust to the semi-dark. I could make out a form reclining on the mattress but the light was too dim and I was too nervous for my initial glance to be anything more than perfunctory. Besides, the form was virtually hidden behind gouts of smoke which billowed up, like Red Indian signals, from the bowl of a pipe. I could hear huge asthmatic heaves, and the bowl of the pipe pulsed with a glowing heap of embers at every full intake of breath. This, I said to myself, is a dope fiend of the first order. Perhaps even the doyen of dope fiends.

A great Aaagh! went up, and the smoke seemed suddenly

to pour from mouth, eyes, and ears, all of which were growing more distinct as I got used to the dark.

'That's more like it,' came a voice from the heart of the fog. 'For a moment there I thought I'd wasted my money. But my toes are just beginning to curl. Another couple of bowls and I should be away.'

Julie laughed uncontrollably. And it was no wonder. Just the fug in the room was getting me off. A hand stretched out, clutching the pipe.

'Here,' the voice said. 'Take this.'

I walked across to the mattress. Then I reached down for the pipe, my eyes following back along the length of the arm to settle briefly on the face. I recognised it instantly. I faltered, quickly trying to determine the state of our relationship. How had we left it? Hadn't confusion surrounded our last encounter at the club? Something about Andy's shoes? I seemed to remember it had. Anyway, it wouldn't be cool to be overly presumptuous. At this stage a simple greeting would do.

'Hi, man,' I offered humbly.

There was a minute when I thought even that had been too familiar, for the face studied mine with a blank, uninterested expression. OK, I thought, everybody wants to be well in with the band, but I didn't deserve this. I wasn't just anybody. I was the genuine article. A fan who really did know the music. The way he'd behaved you'd have thought he was Miles or somebody. It wasn't as if he played the trumpet or sax, he was only the bassist. I was beginning to feel angry and hurt when the face relaxed.

'Well, well,' he said. 'If it isn't ole snakeskin. He of the shoes. He of the pronounced appreciative grunt.'

He broke off to imitate me imitating Errol, then said: 'It's always a pleasure to meet a true aficionado.'

I nodded sheepishly, still not entirely sure of his attitude. Then I sucked on the pipe. I sucked hard but it was out. I went on smiling inanely, trying to make a mental note of the word he'd used so that I could look it up later. At the same time I fumbled for matches. Eventually, I got the pipe going, and inhaled greedily. I could tell there was no tobacco in it. On my second hit the tide swept in, whipped my feet from under me, and I slid away. I passed Julie the pipe, and manoeuvred myself to her cushions.

'Lord,' I said. 'What the hell was *that*?'

It was stronger than anything I'd had before.

'That,' said the bassist, 'is what we call manna from heaven.'

I responded immediately.

'In that case,' I said deadpan, 'hi, Manna.'

Then I pitched into the big league. But it wasn't so big really. At least not too big for somebody who mingled at ease with musicians and dealers, travellers and artists.

I had my stash now. A whole ounce, there in my drawer. I kept on getting it out. I sifted it. I cut it all up the way you were supposed to.

It made me feel good just knowing it was there, nestled against my socks and scants.

My own stash!

Enough for thirty, perhaps even forty joints. On that I could be high for a year.

12

Ah, but how quickly it went when you were in the big league!

'Sure, you can rely on Ned "The Bomber" Selby to come through!'

'Hi, Ned. Come on in. No, I haven't. Oh, *you* have. Wow, that's great, man. I'll pay you back later, you know I will. Can you leave me a little, just enough for a roll?'

'Of course! No trouble! We beats should stick together. All for one, and one for all.'

Pretty soon I was down to my last few joints. But I didn't care. Easy come, easy go. As long as the man was holding I was all right. Next time I bought two ounces, sold a little on the side. A quid deal here, a quid deal there.

The big league.

A true aficionado.

I was hardly ever at home now so I didn't see much of the

Minister or Mary. If I did run into them it was always the same old story. The Minister would rant on at me about time: time running out, or slipping away, wasted time, lost time, time waits for no man, time and chance, marking time, time was, time is and time ever shall be. I'd just smile at him with infinite patience. What is this problem with time? Spontaneity, the creative principle exist outside of time. Can't you see I'm trying to catch time in the act, in the present? He couldn't. Nor could Mary. She worried about my red eyes, the smell in my room.

'You're smoking too much,' she'd say.

I couldn't help laughing at that.

'I smell those funny cigarettes. Why on earth do they have to be French?'

Ah, Mary, they go with my coffee, they go with my jazz. They serve to remind me of the Left Bank, a place which I've never seen, but which I know is my spiritual home.

In fact my fondness for the Left Bank didn't endure. The morning Andy and Julie went I got into work fully expecting to be given Andy's job on the machine. I reckoned it was mine by rights. After all, I was doing three lunch times a week already. I was trained. I had my own white jacket. Besides, who else could possibly do it?

The new manager was the thin, red-headed man with the neat beard sitting in the proprietor's office when she finally summoned me later that day.

'We need permanent employees, regular people,' he told me curtly. 'White shirts, black ties.'

It took me all of a minute to work out I was being given the push.

'I'm sorry, Ned,' the proprietor said. 'You can finish the week, but the Captain here is employing new staff, new ideas.'

Right, I thought to myself bitterly, this is what happens when people go gallivanting about. The world of convention moves in. Sod the Left Bank, we beats should stick together.

I was still peeved when Andy's card arrived. On one side was the Van Gogh self-portrait, the one with the hat and the bandage. On the other, the address of a Paris hotel. It was my last day at work so I didn't pay too much attention. I just read it once, glanced at the picture, then shoved it away in a drawer.

But it left me irritable and tense. At work that afternoon I began to feel as if I was heading back to square one. Unemployment loomed. I had no money, very little dope. I could stand most other privations, except hunger perhaps. But life without dope would be, well, just as it had been before.

Life before dope. What a strange notion. Was it even possible? I vaguely remembered musical evenings, the TV, lights out, thwarted liaisons with fish-eating Germans. But was that life, or some pale imitation? Surely I wasn't zeroing back to all that?

Never! For us beats there was no way back, only an endless series of nows. What did I care if I'd lost my job? There were plenty of jobs. I'd soon find another. Just scan the newspapers, ask around. All I needed to do was to keep out of the Minister's way until I could pay my rent. I wasn't about to suffer his moment of triumph, the expectant look, the knowing nod, the outstretched hand.

'Well?'

'Well, what?'

111

'Haven't you got something for me?'

'Ah, the rent. Of course. I haven't forgotten.'

'Nor have I.'

'I can see that.'

'All right then, where is it?'

'I was wondering . . . '

'Yes?'

'If I could let you have it next week?'

The hand would drop, a flicker of a smile would appear on the face.

'This is the real world, my lad. No quarter given.'

'I haven't got it now.'

'No?'

'No.'

'What's the problem? Bad management? Too much gallivanting about? It's hardly a king's ransom.'

'All I need is a little time.'

'Time, you say! Time! I thought you and your creative principle existed outside of time. In the here and now. Well, this is the here and now. So let's have your rent.'

'I told you I haven't got it. I lost my job.'

'What do you mean *lost* your job? People lose money. Things. They don't lose jobs. They get fired from their jobs.'

'OK, so I got fired from my job.'

'Oh, so you got *fired* from your job.'

'I just said that.'

'The thinking man's washer-up! How can this be?'

'New staff, new ideas.'

'Tell me, what can follow such a glittering career in the catering trade?'

'Another job I suppose.'

'Ach, what in? You're a fool, boy.'

Yes, I could certainly do without that. For two days I made myself scarce. First thing Saturday morning I bought the local newspaper, then spent a couple of hours methodically reading through the job vacancy columns. There were plenty of fruit pickers, cleaners and dishwashers needed. Also labourers and waiters. But there wasn't a single panty-handler required anywhere. With my previous experience that seemed a pity. On the other hand, perhaps it was just as well. I wasn't sure how I could have broken the news to the Minister.

'I'm devoting my life to panties, father.'

Hardly!

I read on, ticking possibilities. But nothing really took my fancy. I was beginning to resign myself to another bout of unseemly toil when I saw it. One word in bold type. 'EXPERIMENT'. After that came two more in smaller print: 'Students wanted'. Then: 'Good pay'. And finally: 'Night-shift'.

I knew I wouldn't have to look any further. My ship had come in. All sorts of wonderful things beckoned. I was on my way, hurtling inexorably towards them.

13

Jubilee – the first name in preserves. That's what the chairman told us the opening night. Fifty of us were massed before him, seated in neat rows, listening to his inaugural address. We hung on his every word. They were spellbinding words, words to weld us together.

'Thank you and welcome,' he said, his eyes searching ours for reciprocal enthusiasm.

He was a grey-faced man with sparse hair and a brown suit. Something about him rang a bell; I thought maybe it was just the content of his speech. I avoided his gaze and looked about me. The ad had stipulated students. I saw big men, rough men, men with tattoos on their arms. There wasn't a student amongst them, not in the sense of O levels anyway. If you counted my two, we might have mustered three between us, but I doubted it. These were all graduates from the university of hard knocks – itinerants, ex-cons, beats. A fraternity of night people.

The chairman was a man on some kind of threshold, a complete fanatic. His voice swelled. The first night shift since the war, he said. A bold step forward, he said. He outlined the benefits of teamwork, told us about the big happy family that was Jubilee. He said there would be a little piece of ourselves on every breakfast table in the land. He finished in ringing tones, urging: 'Go forth and prosper.'

Christ, I stammered to myself in a flash of recognition, old man Williams. I'd been to prep school with his son, Harry. Not a fat boy, but definitely podgy.

Someone along from me belched. That pierced the magic a little, but Williams was totally oblivious, lost in the romance of jam. He beamed at us for a second, then, with a fluttering motion of his hand, dismissed the assembly.

'Bollocks,' muttered the giant next to me, disgustedly lurching to his feet.

'My sentiments entirely,' I said, eager to make his acquaintance.

The man threw me a swift suspicious glance.

'What are you?' he asked. 'One of them fuckin' students?'

'Who me?' I replied. 'Do I look like one?'

'Yep,' he sneered. 'Fuckin' Einstein.'

I managed a grim smile.

We walked through to the main building, a vast neon-lit room filled with machines. A man with a white coat and a bright manner directed us to our stations. I found myself on the corner of a conveyor belt. The man in the coat explained. Gesticulating towards various machines before and behind me, he said:

'Back there, the jars are put on the belt. They go upside down through the steriliser then emerge and pass you, turning arse over tit, if you'll excuse my French, then enter

115

the vat which fills them with jam. What you have to do is check for breakages. If a cracked or damaged jar runs into the vat, it will explode. You whip them out of the line before that happens . . . '

'Is that *all*?' I asked confidently.

'All!' he repeated, amazed at the question. 'Why, the smooth efficiency of the whole operation depends on your eagle eye and manual dexterity, my lad. Every mistake costs Jubilee dear.'

'Don't worry,' I said, tapping my nose. 'You can rely on me. I have this sixth sense.'

The supervisor seemed pleased with my attitude. He nodded, spun on his heels and went off to my new-found friend on the vat. I watched them exchange a few words, then the supervisor continued his tour. My friend came over. This time he extended a hand.

'Len,' he announced.

'Ned,' I answered, my voice struggling against the power of his grip.

'Well, Einstein,' he went on. 'How does it feel?'

I looked down at my bruised hand, flexing the fingers.

'I don't think anything's broken,' I said flatly. 'Crushed, dislocated, but not broken.'

Len roared, throwing his huge head back. Flipping a fist into my chest, he said:

'There's nothing I like more than a man with a sense of humour. Even if he is a fuckin' student.'

I tittered manically.

'Me neither,' I said.

'So how does it feel?' he asked again.

I had no idea what he was talking about.

'Pretty good,' I said, playing it safe.

'OK, we're agreed, then?' he added.

I nodded slowly.

'I'll just give you the word. Then we all get lucky.'

He winked, and sauntered back to the vat.

Just then Williams appeared. I ducked my head, straining my features into a hideous grimace. Even so Williams pegged me.

'Selby,' he exclaimed. 'Ned Selby.'

'Hello, Mr Williams,' I said.

'Well, well. Fancy seeing you here. Where are you now? Oxford? Cambridge?'

'Just taking a year off,' I told him. 'Before I decide.'

'Best time for it,' he said. 'Right after school. A little work experience, travel – they broaden the mind. Harry's at Oxford, you know.'

'I knew he'd go far,' I said.

'How's your father?' Williams asked.

'He's fine,' I said.

'Still playing golf?'

I nodded.

'I must call him up for a game one of these days. You used to be a bit of a player yourself, didn't you, Ned?'

'Some time ago,' I said. 'Not any more.'

'Don't let it slip,' he advised, shaking his head seriously. 'Plenty of business done on the golf course, you know.'

He lingered for a moment longer, then said: 'Well, Ned, happy to have you aboard.'

I thanked him.

'Give my regards to your father,' he said.

I said I would.

Then he was off on his rounds, mingling as all good managers must, getting to know the workforce. I didn't dare look at Len. I felt his eyes boring into the back of my head. When I glanced up, he waved.

'Fuckin' Einstein,' he cried amiably. Then he said, 'Be ready when I give you the nod.'

For five minutes I turned his words over in my head. How does it feel? Be ready? The nod? I racked my brains, trying to work out what he meant. Impossible. I'd heard about men like him: minds impaired by years of gruelling labour. Just humour him, Ned. I winked, I waved, I gave him the thumbs-up. Good old Len. Already we had a fine thing going. Sooner or later I'd get some semblance of sense out of him.

Meanwhile Williams had gone up to his office, a slightly raised glass box at one end of the room. He seemed to survey us from above. Then he did something with his hand. The whole room kicked. There was a grinding of gears. The belt in front of me shuddered, hesitated, then started to roll. Williams lifted his arms triumphantly, clasped them together over his head. We were off and running. Jubilee's first night shift since the war jolted into action.

The job was an absolute cinch. Jars sped by, thousands of them. To begin with I kept my eyes peeled, then I called up my sixth sense. Pretty soon I didn't even have to look. It got so's I could feel the damaged jars coming.

I played games with myself to make the night interesting.

'Ned, give the panel a little piece of mime, will you please?'

'Certainly, Eamon.'

I sang songs. I acted out movies. I even made up one of my own. A young jazz musician's epic struggle for recognition. It had everything: early failure; eventual triumph, untimely death. The Ned Selby Story. About the time 'Ned Lives'

118

started appearing on walls there was a loud plop. My first mistake.

Automatically the belt faltered, stopped. I looked round sheepishly. The man in the white coat came striding towards me, a weary expression on his face.

'What happened?' he asked softly.

He seemed like a kind man, a reasonable man, probably a family man, maybe even a man with worn carpets and home-made lamp standards. I didn't have the heart to tell him about the Ned Selby Story, about all the wan-faced girls putting fresh flowers on my grave, chipping souvenirs from my tombstone.

'A temporary lapse,' I explained apologetically.

He didn't bite, just hung his head sadly. The he told me about goals, how most people had them. He had them. Jubilee had them. He said his and Jubilee's were inextricably linked. Forty-nine thousand jars of jam every night, ten thousand more than the two day shifts. Exactly the number necessary to make the shift viable, to keep him in his job. He wanted my help, he said. No more sixth sense, just eyes. Aye, I said.

He walked off to organise the cleaners. I watched him go, a man bowed down by ambitions, responsibilities, and debts. Ah, life, I mused. The meek shall inherit the earth. There was a sharp tap on my arm. I turned and looked up into Len's untroubled, grinning face.

'Fuckin' Einstein,' he said. 'You read my mind. I was just getting set to give you the nod.'

Here we go again, I thought.

The men began drifting away from their places, gingerly heading for the canteen. Len's eyes followed them appreciatively.

'How does it feel?' he asked. 'There's always a weak link.

And you're it.'

It again. What the hell was *it*?

Len glanced at the factory clock.

'I think we're good for at least half an hour,' he said. 'By the time they've cleaned out the vat, replaced the jam. Oh yes, a nice little break.'

He slapped me hard on the shoulder.

'Course,' he said. 'Mustn't overdo it. Once or twice in the night's enough.'

Then suddenly I understood. The whole process really did depend on me. If I shut my eyes for a moment, plop! I felt that awesome surge. It. The power.

'It feels great, Len,' I told him.

He lifted me out of my stool.

'I knew it would,' he said, laughing.

So there I was, a nightworker. A man with two O levels forswearing the life of the mind, using his hands in honest, humble toil, mixing with other men of hands, men with callused hands. Len, the salt of the earth, bulwark of the nation's industrial wealth.

'Hello, Len.'

'Fuckin' Einstein, what's up?'

Hadn't it always been this way, a few visionaries teaming up with men of action?

The weeks passed easily. It might have been two or ten for all I cared. What with the grass and the weird hours the whole world seemed to go into reverse. Most of the time I

120

was in a kind of trance. I got up when everybody else was going to bed; I went to bed when everybody else was getting up. It was a perfect arrangement. Of course, it wasn't what the Minister had in mind for his one and only, nor did the job have the obvious ups of panty handling, but by and large the Bomber was happy.

A couple of times a night Len and I would bring Jubilee's manufacturing might to an abrupt standstill, but we were subtle about it and nobody suspected. Nod, plop! It was just another accident. A few were unavoidable. And the shift was comfortably achieving its quota. So off we'd troop, out into the balmy September nights for a smoke and a sandwich. I'd sit on a loading pallet out of the way of the rest of the men, light up, gaze at the night sky, and go on doing what I did over the jars: dream, plan, invent great times for myself, momentous events, stupendous sights, visions I'd take to my grave. All of it was there, I knew, waiting around the corner just as Jack said it would be, that moment I'd felt in the club when everything was about to arrive and I'd know everything for ever.

Len seldom joined me for these unofficial breaks. I didn't know where he went, nor did I ask. I simply relished these opportunities to top up on grass, get high for the rest of the night. Sometimes I wondered about putting it to him, introducing him to the magic of the weed, but I always thought better of it for in my heart of hearts I understood we beats had to be careful. Drug, dope, reefer – these words could stir up ferocious prejudices in even the most mutinous of breasts.

One night I was half-dozing out on my pallet, embellishing the Selby saga with one more heart-warming episode in the life of a young jazz musician. The combo's van was stuck in the snow, hopelessly lost, and I was scanning the sky for the Pole Star, the one beyond the Plough, so that we could at least head north when we eventually broke free. I was shovelling and scanning when the unmistakable sounds of hard effort fetched into my mind. Not from me; not from my bassist; not from my drummer. Not from anyone in my epic.

'Shit.'

There it was again. I got up. Silently I strolled the full length of the factory wall to a corner far away from the light cast through the doors and windows. I turned. I stood watching. I could see Len, his van parked in a hidden siding. The doors were open and he was throwing crate after crate of jam in at the back. Amused, I went on looking, then uttered a kind of growl of discovery. Len whipped round, crouching aggressively. Then he recognised me. His breath whistled out.

'Fuckin' Einstein,' he said. 'I thought you was the rozzers.'

He stood up quickly, then he said:

'Now that you're here, why don't you help?'

Just for a second I hesitated. I had no qualms about what he was doing – that was all good grist to the mill. Nevertheless, something inside me veered.

'C'mon,' he said, his impatience obvious. 'Perks of the job. Everybody's doing it.'

I went over to where he stood, shifting the crates with him one at a time into the van. It didn't take long to finish. When we were done Len locked up.

'Little pieces of ourselves,' he said with an air of great satisfaction. 'That's what the old bastard told us. Well, I get a shilling a piece.'

'I knew you couldn't be that crazy about blackcurrants,' I said, grinning.

'Nah,' he replied. 'I've got outlets.' Then he threw me a

probing glance. 'There's a few bob in it for *you* now.'

I felt uneasy shaking my head, but I managed to convince him that what he was doing was fine by me, I just didn't want to be involved myself.

'Fuckin' students,' he grimaced. 'Skivin' off grants, livin' at home.'

'Yep,' I laughed, playing along. 'And don't forget holidays. Months of them. I only work here because I'm an eccentric.'

Len went on giving me the nod, and I went on letting an occasional cracked jar escape my attention, but neither of us referred again to the incident. I imagine he continued his activities for he still disappeared during our irregular breaks and I only saw him when he returned to his place at the vat. His perks were his affair, not mine. Besides, soon after that night I got almost entirely absorbed in a perk of my own.

14

Pearl was her name. One Monday she was there on my station, a gem, a jewel, a vision in white. In fact the whole room was filled with women in white. I stood at the door dumbfounded. For a second I thought I'd gone mad. They said it could happen: murder, insanity, death – an inevitable progression, the end for all dope fiends.

Ribald comments rang in my ears:

'Over 'ere, ducky!'

'Blimey, look what the cat dragged in.'

Where on earth was Len? And all the others? My eyes searched the building. I saw the office, the canteen. The machines still looked the same.

'What you got in your pocket, sonny?' a voice asked.

'A handkerchief,' I snapped back.

Awful mocking laughter swelled up around me. I started backing away, then my eyes lit on the company clock. Nine!

It said nine! Somehow I'd got an hour ahead. This was the earlier shift. Relief burst out of me in a shrill cheep, then I moved forward in the direction of the canteen past so many deft hands, teasing faces. Without stumbling I went, smiling, bowing all the way, thank you ladies, very funny, much obliged. And that's when I saw her, a nymph, an angel, sitting on my stool. My heart soared, I felt weak, my tongue went thick in my mouth. It was love, love at first sight. She was singing to herself as I passed. I could see her lips move, full lips over small white teeth and livid gums, a sweet voice which sounded thin competing with the familiar clatter of the jars. I paused, listened.

'Come fly with me, let's fly, let's fly away.'

Oh yes! Anywhere. The Left Bank, Rio, Bognor. Now, without a moment's delay! Spellbound, I lingered for five choruses. I wanted to break into wild applause. Then she'd turn, smiling warmly.

'You like Frank?' she'd ask in a sultry voice.

'Frank,' I'd exclaim. 'Christ, I'm his greatest fan.'

But she just stared at the conveyor belt, her body swaying slightly to the throb of the beat only she heard, her head turning this way and that as her eyes flicked over the passing jars. Wonderful! Her blonde hair was piled up in a massive hive, her legs, encased in seamed tan stockings, were wrapped around the lower rung of her stool. It was my stool! Our stool! We had yet to speak, but already we had things in common. Two things. Music and furniture. What a start! I tried to approach her but I was rooted to the spot, and words were trapped in my throat. Suddenly the factory whistle blew and I was engulfed in a flurry of women heading for the canteen and locker rooms. They shrieked with delight, nudging one another.

'I like your baby brother, Pearl,' I head one of them say as

125

the girl climbed down from her stool.

But I didn't care for she smiled before she was lost in the crush. Pearl! How appropriate! How precise! Rare, exotic, aglow from a lustre within. She even looked a little like Brigitte. Not a dead ringer, but there were certainly similarities. The hair, the lips, perhaps even the legs. Where had I been until now? Who had I been with? Martha? Agate? They just didn't compare. Agate — I laughed at the double irony. Oh, there'd be musical evenings once more, but what music, what songs!

The night was interminable now. And I was not at my best. I was blind, a fool for love. The jars sped by in a blur. I couldn't distinguish one from another. So many cracked jars exploded into the vat that Len grew concerned.

'What's up, Einstein?' he asked. 'You ill?'

I nodded.

'Yes, Len,' I said. 'A fever.'

'You look all right,' he said sharply.

I sighed.

'The inner man,' I said.

'Bollocks,' he replied, his voice rising. 'I'll give you a fever if you go on screwing up. I don't want you replaced.'

'That's the title of a song,' I said dreamily.

'What is?' he asked.

'You give me fever.'

I fancied I could hear that sweet voice belting out a verse or two.

'What's that got to do with it?'

I smiled indulgently.

'Everything,' I said.

126

Len's eyes searched mine. After a moment he said: 'You've got a bleedin' rut on.'

His voice spilled over with outrage. Poor old Len. A man of hands, of callused hands. How could I explain the finer sensibilities to him?

'Yes,' I said simply. 'That's one way of putting it.'

'The sooner you get your leg over the better, then,' he told me. 'Keep this up and we'll all be out of a job.'

The supervisor tackled me too.

'Quota,' he muttered morosely. 'We mustn't forget the quota.'

Somehow I managed to keep it down to seven stoppages. But it was hard, for all night I worked on the Selby story, adding scenes, making changes. Suddenly there was a spot in the combo for a female vocalist. I auditioned dozens of them. Some had voices but no looks. Some had looks but no voices. I was close to despair when in walked this blonde. Bouffant hair, tall, striking. The moment she sang, hearts melted. A humble working girl. A star.

Next night I was two hours early. I couldn't help myself. But I didn't enter the factory immediately. I paced the perimeter road, suddenly self-conscious, shy. I couldn't believe it. A snivelling adolescent, afraid to walk past a bunch of women. I lectured myself. Come on, Ned, pull yourself together, my lad. They don't call you the Bomber for nothing. Think of the combo. The world is waiting. Take a deep breath. Fix the expression. Walk tall.

I marched in by the massive doors. There they all were. The same white figures.

'Oooh, Gregory, Gregory, give us a peck.'

Ridiculous! I didn't even look like the man. The hoots went up. I took them all in my stride, the smile glazed on my face. There she was again. A miracle. I walked down a corridor of comments, whispers and giggles. I stood behind her back, the white coat tight across her shoulders, her coiffure a marvel of pins and back combing and lacquer. Did she know I was there? She must have done. But she was singing. I picked out a middle eight:

'I didn't want to do it, but all the time you knew it . . . '

Such a repertoire!

'Hello,' I said.

There was a loud plop. The belt shuddered to a halt.

'Now look what you've gone and done,' she said. 'We've got a quota, you know.'

I didn't know where they came from, but up they rose, foolish words:

'An accident,' I said. 'A few are unavoidable. If there's any trouble I'll speak to Williams.'

'Williams?' she asked.

'Yes,' I said. 'Old man Williams. I went to prep school with his son Harry. Not a fat boy but definitely podgy.'

She just gaped at me.

'You must be one of them students,' she said. 'On nights.'

'Yes,' I said expansively. 'A little work experience broadens the mind.'

'Bloody students,' she said with some of Len's original disdain.

'Of course,' I said rapidly. 'I'm not really a student. A student of life perhaps.'

I knew I'd lost her. She started turning away, back to the conveyor belt.

'More of a musician really.'

I don't know what possessed me to make such a wild

claim. Desperation probably. The vast audience of sniggering women and Pearl's increasing lack of interest. I knew I had to do something to regain the initiative. Now I was stuck. Pearl turned back, suddenly all ears.

'Yes,' I burbled. 'A small combo, nothing too professional. We're only rehearsing right now. We need a singer, a female vocalist. Old standards with a jazz flavour – Sinatra, Judy Garland.'

Her face lit up.

'Frank!' she exclaimed. 'I'm his greatest fan.'

What a mess!

I nodded enthusiastically, all the while wading further out of my depth.

'Perhaps you'd like to audition?' I heard myself ask. 'We could talk about it some time.'

She pondered for a moment.

'Maybe I would,' she said at last.

'When?' I demanded. I could just see a supervisor moving in. Not the one from my shift, but a woman, one with a resolute walk, obviously a woman with goals.

'Saturday,' I offered.

I think Pearl nodded, but I may have imagined it.

'Twelve thirty, outside Woolworth's,' I blurted urgently.

Pearl gazed round at her friends. One or two giggled encouragement. Then she turned back to me.

'All right,' she said.

'My name's Ned,' I finished.

Then I was off, out of the building. I roamed the grounds for an hour, making myself scarce until the night shift began.

It was three thirty on Saturday afternoon before Pearl finally got to it.

'Where's the audition then?' she asked.

I'd been stalling for hours. I was tired, still unused to the change from nights to days at the weekends. And I'd known it would eventually come down to this. She was avid for fame. A small-town girl eager to make a name for herself. We'd spent over an hour doing her mum's shopping. I didn't even do that for Mary, let alone anybody else. But I'd queued in the butcher's, queued in the grocer's. Two pounds of sausages, a pound of liver, potatoes, three veg. Now, the moment I dreaded.

'First things first,' I bluffed. 'We have to get to know one another if we're to work together. Let's go for a walk.'

'Where?' she asked.

'Down by the river,' I said. 'I know a nice little meadow.'

'I'm not walking on grass in these heels,' she protested, pointing at her white stilettoes. 'Besides, the liver will run.'

I stopped for a moment, racking my brains.

'Let's go for tea,' I said. 'Afternoon tea.'

'Tea?' she asked.

'Yes,' I said. I remembered a place where the Minister and Mary went in their carefree younger days. By now it would be the haunt of students, queers and Germans.

'At the Doreen,' I went on. 'They have a three piece: drums, bass, piano. Nothing special, not jazz. We can have cream buns, waltz a little if you like.'

Waltz? She just stared at me. This was the era of the twist. Even Frank was doing it.

'Don't worry,' I said brightly. 'It's all very modern. Full of students, Germans and queers.'

I could tell from her face that she didn't like any of them.

'You'll love it,' I said. 'It'll take the weight off your feet.'

I bustled her along, taking charge, giving her no chance to refuse. It wasn't far. In a minute or two we entered a shop selling fresh bread and cakes. We walked to the back, then climbed some stairs which opened up into a large foyer with a hall beyond. It had a waxed parquet floor with tables set around it. The trio was already playing, the kind of band you'd hear at golf club evenings. It wasn't bad if you wanted to dance the old-fashioned way, clutching your partner. Right now that didn't seem such a bad idea. Pearl looked marvellous, white shoes, tight blue dress, nail varnish. She held one bag of groceries, I held the other. A few middle-aged couples attempted a quick-step out on the floor, not a student in sight. But for the clothes, it could have been Victor Sylvester at the Carlton Rooms, Maida Vale, London. My heart sank, but Pearl smiled, her lips moving. A waitress in a black frock and lace pinny led us to a table about ten feet from the band. I ordered tea for two. Pearl shrieked happily.

'That's what they're playing,' she laughed.

I hadn't noticed.

Suddenly she was singing along:

'Tea for two, and two for tea
Me for you, and you for me . . . '

It would be wrong of me to suggest she was directing the lyrics at me. She wasn't. She was in a world of her own. A short high-pitched cough to clear her throat, then the words and melody sang out, clear as a bell. To begin with I was embarrassed. She sang loudly, attracting attention. But the strange thing was she was good.

'You're good,' I told her once she'd finished. 'A little raw round the edges, but nothing we can't easily sort out. Just keep on practising.'

131

She did.

The band started up again.

'Grab your coat and get your hat . . . '

Only the chocolate eclairs that came with the tea stopped her. One, two disappeared. Then she was at it again, as soon as the plate emptied:

'You are my lucky star . . . '

Finally the band began to get interested. I saw the drummer winking at her, showing off by twirling his brushes. I thought that was a bit ripe. After all, she was with me. And he wasn't even young. He kept twirling those brushes, nodding, a big grin on his face. Was that Pearl winking back, or a nervous tic I hadn't previously spotted?

I sat through another song, growing more and more agitated. Then a comforting thought shot into my head. I could tell her she wouldn't have to audition after this. She'd be over the moon. Maybe I'd get that walk in the meadow after all. I perked up at once. I was about to inform her of her immense good fortune, thinking that if the worst came to the worst I could always work something out with my friend the bassist, when the trio began to pack up. I saw two of them confer for a minute, then the drummer stepped down from the stand. Next moment he was looming over our table.

'Hello,' he said, mostly to Pearl. 'Has anybody ever told you you've got a great voice?'

The oldest line in the book! Where did he think he was going to get with that one? Soon he'd be telling her she ought to turn pro!

'Have you ever thought about turning pro?' he asked.

I stared at the floor, my eyes settling on the two bags of

132

groceries. One of the brown paper carriers was starting to tear, with damp patches seeping along the bottom. The liver was beginning to bleed. It wasn't the only thing.

'Ever since I was a kid,' I heard Pearl cry out happily.

I raised up my head as best I could. The drummer was pointing at me.

'What does your brother think?'

'He's not my brother,' Pearl laughed.

But her next line sunk me completely.

'He's a musician too.'

Now I was doomed, with no graceful mode of escape. Maybe I could pull out one of my turns, call on the cupboard again. I came up for air. Then immediately wished I hadn't.

'What instrument?' the drummer asked.

'Bass,' I gasped.

'Let's get together some time,' he offered, one musician to another.

But he couldn't fool me with all that musical fraternity stuff. I knew what he wanted. Yet all I could do was back-pedal.

'Oh, I don't know,' I stammered. 'I don't think you'd want to really. I'm only practising at present. It's just a hobby . . . I only do it for fun.'

My voice trailed away as he lost interest.

'Listen,' he said, turning to Pearl. 'I'd like to give you a trial. We've auditioned dozens of girls, but none of them right. I think you'd work out well. Will you give it a try?'

He handed her a card, then just to keep it fair gave me one too.

'I'm Bert,' he said proudly.

I read the card:

The Bert Black Trio

133

Parties – Reasonable Rates
Evenings – Weekends

Very snappy.

Pearl gripped his card in one of her hands, and gazed up, all misty-eyed.

'I think I will,' she said, throwing me a distinctly hostile glance.

'Please,' the drummer urged. Then he held out his hand, and shook hers lingeringly.

'By the way,' he said. 'What's your name?'

'Pearl.'

'Perfect!' he beamed. Then to me he advised: 'Go on practising.'

I would have kicked him, but he was already gone. I fumed, only vaguely aware of the chink of glass and cutlery as the waitresses began to clear up.

There was a long silence. Pearl pulled a small mirror from her handbag and examined herself approvingly.

'Bert!' I spat. 'Fucking Bert . . . '

'Nothing wrong with Bert,' she said, still gazing into the glass. 'That's my dad's name.'

Yes, I thought, it would be.

'What I mean is . . . ' I struggled, ' . . . well, what does your dad do?'

Pearl put her mirror away, and looked at me sharply.

'He doesn't do anything,' she said. 'He's dead.'

Somehow I knew she'd say that. Clumsily, I apologised at once.

'It's all right,' she said. 'It was a long time ago. When he was alive he worked on the railway.'

'Ah!' I jumped. 'Now you can see what I mean. Bert's a terrific name for a man who works on the railway, but who ever heard of a drummer called Bert? Bert Krupa . . . Bert Rich – it just sounds daft.'

'Sounds all right to me,' she said tetchily. 'Anyway, I liked him.'

'He was OK,' I said. 'But you know what he really wanted, don't you?'

'A walk in the grass,' she said. 'Like you.'

Suddenly she was one of those girls from the Crucible: ridiculous hair, white shoes, daubed make-up.

'Besides,' she went on. 'You're the one with the hobby. I thought you were serious.'

'I am serious, honestly,' I said quickly. 'But I don't just play with anyone. And never with a drummer called Bert. We wouldn't have the same musical tastes. I'm talking about jazz, Billie Holiday . . .'

'Never heard of him,' she sniffed.

'Her,' I corrected. 'Call yourself a singer? I'm beginning to have second thoughts.'

'I already have,' she said.

She got up clutching her mum's groceries.

'Is that all you want to do with your life?' I shouted. 'Golf clubs, afternoon teas, parties. You'll regret this. All sorts of wonderful things beckon.'

But I was shouting at the air. She waddled away on her too-high heels, a small-town girl, no vision, no style. The combo could do without a singer, at least for the time being. I sat there pondering for a moment. Bert Black, what the hell did he know? Bert and Pearl. Pearl and Bert. Yes, they deserved each other.

I went home. For the rest of the weekend I slept. Come Monday I clocked on at the usual time.

135

15

I was six weeks into the job, on my way home when it happened. They came at me from all sides. I was outnumbered three to one. I didn't stand much of a chance. In my bicycle basket were two pots of jam, the first raspberry of the shift. I was taking them home for Mary, a small token of my appreciation for all the packed lunches she'd made me.

'You know who we are,' one of them cried, flailing his arms as he burst out of a hedge.

For a moment I hadn't the least idea. Birdwatchers, perhaps. I swerved to a halt, dismounting. They crowded round, blocking all chance of escape. One of them flipped back his lapel, flashing a badge.

'Security,' he rasped.

'Ah.'

I grinned to myself. At the end of the track I could just see cars leaving by the factory gates. Len was in one of them, along with six pairs of new overalls, four folding chairs from the company canteen, and enough jam to supply all of the town's cafés for a month. I didn't think I had anything to hide. Laughing, I thrust out my wrists for the cuffs.

'I'll come quietly,' I said. 'It's a fair cop. I've got two pots of raspberry.'

There was a muffled whoop, then one of them pounced on my basket. Holding the two jars aloft, he went into a kind of victory dance.

'You're in trouble, my lad,' he sang. 'This is a serious offence.'

Two pots of jam! He had to be kidding.

'Come off it, men,' I protested. 'It's hardly a king's ransom.'

But I was expected to quake. They wanted guilt. They wanted remorse. I dropped my head, faking it.

'What made you do it?' one asked in a wounded tone. 'You don't sound like a run-of-the-mill worker to me.'

What could I say? Perks of the job. Everybody was doing it. Or should I tell him about the warm feeling which crept up on me when I was shelling my boiled egg during the early morning break? Nobody hard-boiled an egg the way your mother did. A thought like that did something to you. Brought a lump to your throat.

'I was only thinking of Mary,' I said.

'Mary?'

'My mother,' I said.

The man was amazed.

'Is that what you call her? No wonder you're in trouble.'

Perhaps I could plead temporary insanity: it was the dope done it, your honour.

But I didn't say anything. I waited. They waited. Then

137

they went into a huddle.

'What happens now?' I asked after a minute.

'This may well be a matter for the police, the courts. It's up to the management to decide.'

'Old man Williams,' I said, nodding.

'You know him?' one of them asked.

'A friend of the family's,' I said.

'Then yours is the worst kind of thievery, stealing from friends.'

He took out a notebook and pencil.

'Selby's the name,' I told him. 'Ned Selby.'

He wrote with some difficulty, moistening the tip of the pencil with his tongue.

'S-E-L-B-Y,' I spelt. 'First name Ned. Sometimes known as the Bomber.'

He took it all down.

'It'll be the sack, possibly prosecution,' he said, snapping the book shut. 'We'll tell you tonight.'

'That's terrible,' I said, bowing my shoulders.

'Crime never pays. You should know that.'

I choked back a smile, remembering the chairs, the overalls, the jam. Then slowly, I looked at each face.

'I've learned my lesson,' I said. 'You're much too clever for me.'

That softened them noticeably. One of them handed me my bike.

'You get along home,' he said. 'No doubt you're tired, and you'll have some explaining to do.'

'Thank you, sir,' I said, trying to sound sick.

They stepped away. I climbed on my bike and rode down the track. Fifty yards on I turned round to wave. The poor fools were clambering back into the hedge.

Mary was in the kitchen when I got home, tidying up after the Minister's breakfast.

'How was your night, dear?' she asked as I opened the door.

'Terrific,' I said. 'We started on raspberry.'

'That's nice,' she said.

'I had something for you, but somebody took it.'

'Never mind, dear,' she said absently. 'It's the thought that counts.'

'That's what I say,' I said.

I went upstairs and made ready for bed, smoking a small one-paper reefer before going to sleep. Half-way through it I started to laugh. I kept seeing men leaping through hedges at me, a whole legion of lookalikes chasing after me as I pedalled away with my swag. Two pots of jam! Suddenly I was Mr Big in the world of illicit preserves. At least Len would appreciate that.

I must have fallen into a doze. I thought I heard a phone ringing somewhere, but I was probably dreaming. Then I heard this low groaning sound. I drifted into that half-sleep, half-waking state but still heard it, a sort of muffled cry that went on and on. I opened my eyes. There, at the foot of my bed, was a horrible apparition! What on earth was it? The ghost of Christmas past? What kind of hideous nightmare was I waking from or to? It – she – was wringing her hands. Lady Macbeth! Gradually my eyes focused. I recognised the features. They were Mary's. But something was dreadfully wrong. A train crash! The Minister struck down in the prime of life! The moaning went on and on, turning over and over, quietly, rhythmically, like a well-tuned motor. Then a few words came out, apparently disconnected.

'Wait . . . wait until your father comes home. Think of the shame. The blinds, I must draw the blinds.'

I rose up. I could tell circumstances required a commanding voice, an imperious manner.

'What's going on here?' I demanded.

The motor droned on, spluttering occasionally now.

'Jazz, girls – where did I go wrong? I tried, God knows, I tried.'

In films you slapped sense into them, but I didn't think I could do that.

'Pull yourself together,' I said, settling back on the pillows for a long wait.

'Thief! Robber!'

What the hell was she babbling about?

'A child of my own . . . two O levels . . . lives in ruins.'

I just lay there listening. Slowly a picture began to emerge. It had me in it. Plus scenes of appalling chaos. This was the end of everything, Mary said. The final straw. Soon there'd be police, arrests, prison. At that very moment the Minister was on his way home to confront me.

So that was it. Old man Wiliams had called up the Minister in London. It was insane. I'd dismissed the morning's incident as a silly charade, a bluff to get the word out to people like Len. Yet it was obvious now that the guards had been serious. I shook my head in disbelief.

'Two pots of jam!' I exclaimed. 'All this fuss over a lousy two pots of jam. Christ, I only took them for you.'

Mary let out a howl of pain, then buried her face in her hands. I had to say something quickly.

'Don't worry,' I said. 'I won't tell *that* to the court.'

She flopped forwards, grabbing the foot of my bed. When she started to shake I grew afraid. But I was angry too. I felt possessed by the spectacle of this weeping woman, responsible for it. Yet at the same time I felt that that responsibility was a monstrous and unfair burden. The world of convention had moved in. The world of spurious authorities with stupid rules and weird priorities. Well, I wanted none of it. I decided I wouldn't wait for the Minister to harangue me with another of his familiar lectures. I'd be out when he came home. As for Mary, there was little I could do. I tried telling her Williams wouldn't press charges. What sort of friend would bring disgrace on the family, I asked.

But it only set off a fresh bout of anguish. We'd be shunned, forced to move out of the area. When she described the effect my behaviour would have on their position at the golf club I lost all patience. I jumped up, bollock naked.

'Cover yourself up,' she cried. 'Have you no shame, no decency?'

'None whatsoever,' I replied angrily. 'I like jazz, Jack Kerouac.'

I grabbed one of his books, thrust it under her nose.

'Ned Selby!' I shouted. 'This . . . this is your life.'

It was the one with the nudes on the front. Mary blanched, and fell into spasm.

'Not for me your golf clubs and fat boys, your prep schools and O levels,' I raved. 'There's more to life than afternoon teas and the Bert Black Trio.'

Mary sucked at the air. I was incensed. I'd never spoken to her this way before, and it shocked even me. Incredulous, one part of me listened. This wasn't just anybody, this was Mary, the woman who hard-boiled my eggs. How could I reduce her to this? I was a fiend, addled by drugs, perverted by books. But the other part of me roared, giddy with the upsurge of anger.

'Two pots of jam,' I cried. 'For these you go into mourning. You're all mad. You, Williams, the Minister – completely nuts.'

Then suddenly Mary went quiet. The moaning stopped. The crying stopped. Suddenly she was eerily calm. She stood up, gazing at me steadily. I'd never seen her like this. She had the tranquil look of someone who has finally surrendered to what was always inevitable. It was even more scary than her usual welter of tears.

'You just don't understand the trouble you're in,' she said sadly. 'The trouble you cause.'

'Rubbish,' I snapped. 'No trouble.'

'Stealing,' she said. 'What's it going to be next? Where will it end?'

'Probably in murder, insanity and death,' I said.

Mary shrugged.

'Well, it's your life,' she said.

'*My* life!' I shouted hysterically. 'I was under the impression it was everybody else's. Yours, the neighbours', fat boys'. I'm the last person it ever belonged to.'

'When have you ever done anything you didn't want to?' she asked firmly.

I expected this sort of stuff from the Minister, but coming from Mary it threw me badly. For a moment I was stuck for words.

'I'm getting dressed, then I'm going out,' I said.

'Don't you think you ought to wait for your father?' she asked.

'What for?' I replied. 'More of the same?'

'You can't avoid him for ever,' she said. 'And what about Mr Williams?'

'What about him?' I barked.

'You're supposed to meet him tonight before you start work.' Then she added, 'That is, if they let you start work, if they don't prosecute.'

At that point she suffered a temporary relapse. Images of

the police gripped her again, and she fled from my room, presumably to close up the curtains. Hurriedly, I finished dressing. I took enough grass from my drawer to roll up a joint, then hid the rest more diligently than usual. Fortunately I didn't see Mary on the way out. By then it was four in the afternoon. One more delay would have held me at home until the Minister returned. I pedalled away from the house in some haste. I didn't much care where I was going, so long as it was quiet, and I could be alone.

Instinctively, I headed for the river. I parked my bike and sat on a bench. Along the banks people walked dogs and fed ducks. It was a perfectly normal evening, but I felt beside myself, seized by a sense of outrage. Anyone with half a brain could see the vast schism between the scale of my act and the scale of the general response to it, yet here I was having to brace myself for a set of awkward interviews with half-mad adults intent on exacting almost divine retribution. There was only one thing for it, I decided. Dope. I whipped out my grass. In a couple of minutes I'd rolled a monster. I sat watching the sun go down, all the while puffing hard. One by one the strollers drifted away, back to their living rooms and TVs, and before long I was alone. I shut my eyes, relishing the gentle transformation. The air hummed softly; the river purled by, a low whisper some distance off. Gradually my mood took on a different aspect. No longer angry, I felt purged, awash with a new benevolence. I seemed to soar above all ordinary concerns. I no longer blamed the Minister and Mary for their ignorance and prejudice. Nor Williams even. I saw more than they did, and seeing more I was able to forgive and forget. Yes, in a humble way I was a prophet, a healer. At last I could embrace my fate. It was the lonely fate of the one who knows. The fate of the seer.

I stayed where I was for another half-hour, then set out for my meeting with Williams. I had no anxieties now. My new-found peace emanated from me, radiant, obvious, able to compose whatever unquiet impulse it might meet with.

I strode confidently in by Jubilee's factory doors, then stood between them emanating. The women of the early shift barely seemed to notice.

'You wouldn't think he'd have the nerve, comin' in 'ere,' one of them said. 'Look at 'im standin' there, as if he owns the place.'

I turned and gave her a jolt. But the unquiet impulse lingered.

'I hear it's the pokey for you, my lad,' she continued. 'Serves you right if you ask me.'

I set off on the long trek past the machines to the office, my new-found peace a trifle ruffled. I approached my stool emanating for all I was worth, but Pearl wasn't on it.

'You won't find Pearl, if that's what you're after,' I was informed. 'She's left.'

The speaker paused, examining my face for a reaction, then laughed.

'Oh yes,' she said. 'All sorts of wonderful things happened. She's getting married. You might say into her job. She sings in her husband-to-be's trio. Bert Black. You must have heard of Bert Black.'

I nodded quickly. I had several unquiet impulses of my own, but managed to contain them.

'Marvellous,' I said deadpan. 'They deserve each other.'

I looked up, peering into the office to see if Williams was there. I half hoped he'd been taken ill, not seriously so, but enough to keep him out of the way for a week or two. There seemed to be nobody about, but as I was looking up somebody tugged at my sleeve.

'He's waiting for you, son,' a voice said.

The supervisor from my shift stood next to me. His stricken eyes delved mine, as if for explanations. Then he sighed sadly.

'This could be the end of night work,' he said. 'And we were meeting the quota too. You just don't know the trouble you've caused.'

That line again. It would try the patience of even the most experienced seer, let alone that of a callow beginner like me. The last vestige of benevolence vanished. I simply felt put upon by these fools. This one acted like a man betrayed, shuffling heavily in front of me, head bowed, shoulders stooped, more hurt than angry. Well, sod him too, I thought. Let's get this over with so we can all get on with our lives.

I plummeted down. I felt trapped, isolated. My last thought at Williams's door was that I wanted my own people again. I wanted rooms, crowded rooms. I wanted coffee and grass, jazz and laughter. But I had no time to pursue it before I was ushered inside. Williams sat at his desk, distraught.

'Selby,' he murmured. 'Ned Selby.'

That was me all right, so I nodded. Then he said it again, shaking his head wearily, speaking in a tone of infinite regret and grief.

'When I heard it was you,' he explained, 'I reacted as if it was my own boy who'd done it.'

I thought that was strange for I'd only seen Williams once in eight years, and I didn't think that made me a part of the family. Still, I could hear the lump in his throat. There was no point in arguing.

'I was disappointed,' he told me. 'I was hurt.' Then he paused, lowering his voice for the kicker.

'And I was angry, too.'

145

He fixed me with his gaze. I fixed him with mine. Suddenly I realised I was supposed to react. I trembled, blinked back a tear.

'I had to ask myself if I was the kind of man who would prosecute one of his own flesh and blood,' Williams went on gravely.

Then he lapsed into another silence, mulling over the moral dilemma. I blinked back a second tear.

'In the end I called up your father,' he said. 'I put the matter to him.'

Thank God for the Minister! He wouldn't let me down. Despite everything I was still his blood.

'He told me to do whatever I deemed fit,' Williams said.

The old bastard, I thought. I was stunned. What kind of heartless brute would abandon his son?

The anger must have seeped into my face, for Williams smiled, almost enjoying himself now. His voice droned on. I did my best to cancel it out, but he kept forcing my attention with questions.

'What made you do it?' he asked.

A dozen insolent answers jumped into my head. Dope, a sudden wild urge, an uncontrollable craving for jam . . .

'I like raspberry,' I replied. 'We started on raspberry.'

'Ach,' he said.

He raised his arms, apparently at a loss.

'Why didn't you come to me?' he asked. 'At Jubilee we're not ungenerous. You could have had any amount at a trade discount.'

Of course, yes. I should have known. Remind me to tell that to Len.

But Williams was off again, this time on Mary's tack. Shame, family, neighbours. He dragged everything in, even the old school tie. Finally, he came to the nub.

146

'You're a very lucky man,' he said. 'I think too much of your parents to press things further. I'm not even going to sack you. But I think you should do the honourable thing.'

The honourable thing? What the hell was the honourable thing? Perhaps I should fall on my sword, take that long walk into the snow. I looked at Williams askance.

'Resign,' he said. 'I think you ought to resign.'

I nodded, but I could tell there was something else.

'Isn't there anything you want to say?'

I just looked at him, my mind a blank.

'How about "I'm sorry"?' he asked.

Sorry? Yes, I was sorry. Sorry for all the interference. Sorry I was no longer high. Sorry I wasn't in town listening to jazz. There were a hundred and one things I was sorry about, but they didn't include two pots of Jubilee jam.

'I'm sorry,' I grunted quickly.

Williams wasn't convinced. For a moment he looked on the verge of opening up the issues again, but then in a low, exasperated voice he asked me to leave. He was on the phone before I got to the door.

'Mr Selby,' I heard.

I didn't pause to listen. Outside the women had finished their shift. I went straight to the lockers to find Len.

He jumped up the instant he saw me.

'Here he comes,' he cried. 'The fuckin' thief of Baghdad.'

I laughed along with the others, and walked over to him.

'Well, Einstein,' he said. 'You really dropped yourself in it. What did they give you? Life?'

'No,' I said. 'The honourable thing.'

'What the fuck's the honourable thing?' he asked.

147

'They told me to resign,' I said.

'Quite right,' he returned quickly. 'Can't have a thief in the workforce. One bad apple . . . '

He winked, clapped me on the back, then asked: 'What are you going to do now?'

'Who knows?' I replied nonchalantly. 'I never make any long-term plans. But there's no sense in hanging around here. I think I'll go into town and get thoroughly pissed.'

Len looked at his watch.

'You better be off then,' he said. 'You've only got an hour before they close.'

I nodded, somehow expecting more.

'By the way,' he asked. 'Where do you drink?'

'The Crucible,' I said.

He screwed up his face.

'I might have known,' he said. 'Students, poofs and Yanks.'

I laughed, then he added:

'Still a drink's a drink. One night I'll come in and see you.'

I smiled for a second, then reached out my hand.

'You do that, Len,' I said. 'It was a good team while it lasted.'

'Yes,' he said cheerfully. 'It was.'

He gave me one of his nods, the kind that meant it was time to send a damaged jar into the vat, then both of us laughed. We shook hands. Then I turned and walked out of the canteen, out of the factory into the night, my short illustrious career with Jubilee, the first name in preserves, at an end.

16

I had to wing it into town. Cycling full pelt, I didn't give myself a chance to dwell on recent events, nor did I allow myself to even anticipate any of the irksome ones that might be pending. Occasionally jumbled images, just flashes really, burst in on me with hints of their contingent irritations – a flash of guilt, a flash of anger – but by pedalling furiously I managed to keep most of these unpleasant feelings a safe distance from me. In fact, as I sped away from Jubilee I was overtaken by a sense of release, and all of a sudden I was swept along in its welcome surge.

'Sod 'em,' I thought happily. 'Sod 'em all.'

I arrrived at the Crucible panting hard, but well in time to suck down a couple of beers. The place was throbbing. It was packed with the usual crowd – poofs, students and Yanks, just as Len said – but over at a table at the back was my bassist friend, Don, along with several others, two or

149

three of whom were unfamiliar. I hadn't seen Don since I started nights so I didn't press myself upon his company, but as I bought a drink he noticed my reflection in the bar mirror and at once stood up to beckon me over.

'Ned,' he shouted warmly. 'Man, I thought we'd lost you.'

'No, man,' I answered, smiling comfortably. 'Nearly, but not quite.'

The word rolled off my tongue again. No raised eyebrows, no peculiar looks, no embarrassed sniggers. God, it felt good. It felt as if I'd arrived home after a long, long trip.

I sat down, nodding at the new faces as I was introduced. Two of them were old friends of Don's, down from London for a visit. And they did look like big-city people, sharply dressed, with three-button jackets, wing-collared shirts, and expensive Anello and Davide boots from the Charing Cross Road. One of them, a poet who was just beginning to make a name in all the best beat circles, wore tinted glasses, with his hair combed forward. For a moment I felt drab beside them, perhaps a little out of my depth, but it didn't last. Don asked what I'd been doing for so long, and once I'd sat down I gave them the whole story. I told it well, embellishing here, exaggerating there, building myself up, telling them about Len and our system, Pearl and Bert Black, finishing up with the great jam robbery and my encounter with Williams. I left out everything involving the Minister and Mary for all those at the table seemed beyond the reach of parents and family and it fleetingly struck me as I spoke that the fact that I wasn't would somehow diminish the grade and quality of my heroic adventures. As it was I made them laugh, and I felt good knowing I could hold my own in fast company.

More people came to the table, including two girls. One was an art student, the spitting image of Rita Tushingham.

150

At first I was convinced she was Tush, then, when it became clear she wasn't, I made the mistake of asking her if anybody had ever remarked upon the astonishing similarity between them. I was still peaking on the discovery of my prowess as a raconteur, and her reaction shook me rigid. Talk about the *grand ennui*!

'What do *you* think, Einstein?' she sneered.

There was laughter round the table, and I froze. It wasn't just the sharpness of her put-down which was upsetting. Her use of that name was a weird and unnerving coincidence which spun me momentarily back to Len and Jubilee, and inevitably to Williams, the Minister and Mary. It didn't stop there, either. I was seized by doubts, vague, alarming doubts, which provoked a sudden whirl of disabling panic. It took me five minutes to recover, five silent minutes during which I felt as if I'd disappeared.

But then time was called and I was quickly caught up in the ensuing arrangements. Eventually all of us went back to Don's. He tagged me outside the pub and, when I realised I was as much a part of the proceedings as anyone else, I felt considerably reassured.

The other girl with us must have been twenty-two or twenty-three. She was a tall, thin beauty with piercing eyes and a disturbingly remote manner. There was something distinctly different about her, though I couldn't quite put my finger on what it was. I thought it was just her age and that experienced air she carried about with her, but as we ambled along Don let it drop that she was a registered addict. He was very casual about it, but it rattled me. I'd never met a junkie before. I kept looking at her, keeping my distance, but watching for signs of that other-worldliness I expected her to exhibit. Sitting a few feet away from her in Don's room, I couldn't help wondering when she would

151

whip out her works and shoot up. She never did, though I was a little leery of the joints she rolled, taking only cautious hits in case they were special, filled with more exotic and unmanageable substances than the usual grass.

Don's room was a good-sized place, but there were at least a dozen of us. Bodies were packed together on the bed and spread out on the floor. I sat next to one of the out-of-town visitors who pulled ready rolls from his wallet, tight little smokes which always came to me first. These I drew on fiercely. The smoke was less harsh on the throat and lungs than I was used to, but stronger, more soporific. He told me it was hash. That was another first. The dope circled, joints appearing from all parts of the room so that I lost track of where they should go to next. Sometimes I had two in my hand at once. I got so stoned I could barely speak. I just lounged, grinning inanely. It was the perfect night for my comeback, definitely building up into one for the books.

After about an hour Don pressed his poet friend to read. There was an immediate rumble of approval and the guy in the dark glasses pulled out a wad of folded papers from the inside pocket of his three-buttoned jacket. I giggled, thinking that he must have been in better shape than I was for I could barely speak, let alone read, but he took it badly, giving me a long angry glare.

'What's the matter?' he asked scathingly. 'Don't you like poetry?'

The force of his aggression wounded.

'Who, me?' I burbled. 'Why, certainly. Yes. I write it myself.'

That was a bad mistake. His lips curled in a sour grin.

'Perhaps we can hear from you when I finish then,' he said.

'No, no,' I replied instantly. 'I'm not prepared.'

'What do you need to prepare?' he asked.

'A defence,' snapped the girl who looked like Rita Tushingham.

I tried to explain why I'd laughed but the words came out haltingly. The more I tried, the more tangled my effort became. I stopped. Everybody was looking at me.

'Be cool, man,' Don instructed.

I shrank back into the bed, beginning to vanish again. This wasn't how it was supposed to be. We beats were supposed to stick together. I wanted to cry out, but the poet was reading now. I couldn't distinguish the words. All I could hear was this low droning voice and people grunting appreciatively in all the right places.

I started to panic. Soon he'd be finished. Then I'd be exposed, open to ridicule. Desperate, I thought I might draw on the nipple poem:

> Her box of nipples
> Erected like a sandwich.

But it didn't sound right. Besides, I didn't think I could spin it out for over an hour. People in the best beat circles wouldn't sit through it. I decided to leave, then realised I couldn't get to the door without causing a serious disturbance. I was trapped. I just lay there decomposing, my hands and feet numb, stuck uselessly out at the ends of my limbs.

Suddenly there was a round of applause. The poet leant back, smoking. I found myself pleading, praying for all I was worth that he wouldn't call on me. I wasn't really a poet. I'd never written a poem in my life. I was a lounger, a drifter. I was a thief of the worst kind. I had two O levels and lived with my parents.

Somewhere I heard a whisper.

'Cop some of this,' it urged.

I looked to my left. The stranger next to me was involved in an elaborate ritual I didn't understand. He had a tiny piece of what looked like earth on the end of a pin. He was putting a match to it. I watched it glow, burning off a heavy perfumed vapour. He waved the glowing ember under my nose.

'Good, huh,' he said.

I breathed in, nodding.

'Smells good, yes,' I muttered.

My voice echoed, reverberating endlessly through a vast hollow chamber. The vapour smelt like incense. It filled my nostrils, my head, my lungs.

The man next to me laughed.

An instant later there was a dull, horrendous thump inside my chest. It flung me upright. Then I was rocking backwards and forwards, gasping.

I heard a snigger.

'The horrors,' a voice mocked. 'He's having the horrors.'

The horrors! Christ, I was dying. I hugged my knees, rocking. Oh God, don't let me die! Still someone laughed. My heart had just burst and the beats were laughing! They were ugly, crazy, and I was going to die in their room. They'd have to dispose of my body. They would drag it out to a car and dump it somewhere. Fiends! Addicts! I was coming up to my last gasp. There! I was gone, finished! Now they could do what they liked.

But I was still rocking, clasping my knees. Somehow I'd come back from the dead.

'You all right?' Don asked.

His voice seemed to come up from the bowels of the earth, rumbling, distorted.

'No,' I moaned, rocking frantically. 'Dying . . . heart attack.'

My voice seemed strange. Everything was strange. Suddenly everything was hideous, alien. Faces had no blood, bodies no bones. People were just leering, shapeless forms of slack flesh.

Every so often my body seemed to flood with a dense warm fluid. It rose up inexorably from my feet, up past my knees, my groin, and my belly. Every time it got to my heart I thought I'd pass out. I kept holding my breath. Each time it ebbed. Each time I survived. Then it would start flooding again.

'You won't die,' Don said. 'It's only the horrors. It happens to the best of us. You'll laugh about this in the morning.'

Morning! What morning? I was all out of mornings. Couldn't he see that?

So this was it, I thought. They said it would happen. If you flouted the world of convention what else could you expect. The big league! An ignominious death in a sordid room surrounded by blobs. Well, I'd made it. They didn't come any bigger.

I wanted to get up, go home. I wanted worn carpets, home-made lamp standards. I wanted to die in my own bed with Mary and the Minister next door. They were good people, kind people. They'd sacrificed everything. If only I wasn't dying I'd make amends. But it was too late now. Oh God, I don't want to die . . .

Somehow I stopped rocking. I pushed myself to my feet. I staggered on limp legs, sweating from the attempt. Then I lurched for the door, bouncing off walls as I went, stumbling over bodies.

'Be cool, man.'

'Go with it, man.'

Words from the void. Dead words, empty and meaningless. I fought my way forwards.

'Why don't you stay and read us your poems?'

The flood rose. I held back my breath. Miraculously it ebbed. I seemed to stand at the door for hours, my hands refusing to obey my instructions. I had about as much control over them as I'd have over the metal callipers in that fairground game, the one where you set out to pick up the prize, but all you ever get is a piece of stale popcorn. My fingers wouldn't grip. They slid on the knob. They weren't the same fingers or hands I'd had with me at Jubilee. Those hands worked. They were good hands, clever hands. But they were also the hands of a thief.

Perhaps I cried out for Don was beside me now.

'Let me do it,' he said.

He wasn't dying so it was easy for him. I watched his fingers circle the knob.

'There,' he said, pulling the door open.

Then I was out in the hall.

'Take it easy,' a voice said. 'You'll be all right.'

A sure sign whenever you hear it. You cough, smile weakly, then a sheet is pulled over your face.

I didn't look back. I shambled downstairs, hugging the wall. At the bottom I came to a door. My legs buckled as I tore at the latch. I felt the flood rising and started to babble. Our Father, Which art in Heaven, hallowed be Thy name. . . . But that was as far as I got. I couldn't concentrate. I tried beginning again, but it was no good. Obviously the devil had me, as he had all dopers, wastrels and jam thieves.

I gave the latch one last despairing heave. Suddenly it flicked open. I spun out into the street, gratefully sucking at the fresh air. But there was no respite. Outside it was pitch black and I'd lost my bearings. I stumbled to the end of the street towards a single lamp on the corner. When I got there I stopped. Instantly the flood rose. Then once again it ebbed. I plodded on. It was like walking down an endless tunnel. I could see myself growing smaller and smaller. I expected to meet gigantic spiders, vast cats. I tried to speed up, whacking my legs with my arms. My footsteps made a deafening clatter. I tried praying again. All I could remember was the line of a hymn, 'Oh hear us when we cry to thee for those in peril on the sea.' It didn't seem to have much to do with my case, but I repeated it over and over as I trudged. I must have walked miles. Several times I was certain I'd circled back on myself. It was hopeless. Anyway, what was the point? Death was death wherever you were. I thought of Mary, I thought of the Minister. Would they grieve? Would anyone grieve? I didn't think so. I was beyond grief, beyond sorrow. There were no more bridges to burn. I was guilty, guilty, guilty.

The word rose with another flood. Then I saw lights, places I recognised. Woollies, Marks and Sparks. Wonderful places filled with sweets and toys, shirts and sweaters. How beautiful it all looked! And I'd never appreciated it. Only in death had I seen the light. What a waste! What a loss!

I pressed on for the Market Square, praying they hadn't moved it. Steeling myself, I turned a corner. It was still there! Cobbles, public toilets, a fountain. I took a deep breath and stepped into the open. Nobody was about except two taxi drivers on the far side, smoking and talking outside their cars. I strode towards them, not small now, a tottering giant. It took ages. I could see their lips move. They were talking about me, discussing whether or not to pick up my fare. One was for it, one against. They argued as I walked. They seemed to know all about me, where I'd been, what I'd done. I couldn't understand it. I kept walking, trying to look normal, but it was hard for I was still in the throes of death. I

157

reached them, trembling. The two men parted, each going to his own car.

'Where to, sir?' asked the first, opening the door.

The car looked like a hearse. I hesitated.

'Where to?' he repeated.

With an immense effort of will I gave my address, and bundled in at the back. My voice sounded remote, not mine. Perhaps I was already dead, already in hell.

The car started. I slumped, clutching my chest, frantically tapping my foot to keep the blood moving. I felt rivers of the stuff pumping. I was certain I'd throw up. Desperately, I fought for my life. I counted, I prayed, I tapped my foot.

'You all right?' a voice asked.

I saw the whites of the driver's eyes in the rear-view mirror.

'You're not going to throw up, or nothing?'

I gagged, swallowing hard.

'Whatsa matter? Been on the drink?'

Weakly, I nodded.

'Happens to the best of us,' the cabby laughed. 'You'll be all right.'

A sure sign whenever you hear it.

I shut my eyes, feeling every bump and rut in the road. The whole of my life flashed before me. How little I'd done, how selfish I'd been! The Minister and Mary would be better off rid of me. I understood that now. But I wanted to see home again – one last time see the clapped-out TV, the radiogram with its back off, all the familiar things I might have cherished. I choked back a sob. I could see my tombstone one year hence, neglected, overgrown with weeds. 'Here lies Ned Selby.' Then what else would it say? Loving son? Scholar? Captain of industry? I could think of nothing worth a mason's fee. I'd leave one of those notes, spidery writing on torn paper: 'Commit my body to an unmarked grave, let not my shameful story stand.'

I felt the taxi slow into a turn. I opened my eyes. We were on my street! The street where I was born, the street with the fat boy on the corner! Ah, if only I'd been fat. A hundred 'if onlys' spun into my brain. Then a fresh panic took me. What if the Minister was waiting? I could just see it. I would open the door, a light would snap on. He'd be standing there, eyes popping, half-lenses sliding down the blade of his nose. I'd grovel. I'd beg. I'd tell him he'd always been right, then I would die at his feet.

'What number did you say, sir?' the cabbie asked.

'Six six six, the sign of the beast.'

Automatically it jumped into my head, but I don't think I said it.

'Ten,' I managed. 'Between eight and twelve.'

The taxi came to a halt. I gazed out of the window. Yes, there they were – lawns, a lilac bush. I fumbled with change, paid, and clambered out. I stood looking at the house. It was a small house, poignant, redolent of countless sacrifices. No lights, and the blinds were drawn. I walked up the path on tiptoe, quiet as I could. Even so, I thought the noise of my passage would wake the whole street. I got to the kitchen door, tried it. I fell inside. Still no light switched on. I felt my way to the hall, to the foot of the stairs, then I pulled myself up by the banisters. Each stair creaked, so many coffins opening and closing. At the top I waited again. Nobody stirred. It was as dark and as quiet as the grave, but soon I'd be used to that. With my last breath rattling in my throat I got to my room. I stretched out on my bed, exhausted. Silently I said my goodbyes, then I crossed my arms on my

159

chest, coughed weakly, and, with one last prayer on my lips, made ready to die.

'Oh hear us when we cry to thee for those in peril on the sea.'

17

Oh what a piece of work is man: two arms, two legs, feet, hands, head, heart, nails, hair. I flexed muscles, shifted limbs. Incredible! I wasn't dead.

I raised myself up, and turned to the mirror. A little pale, drawn round the eyes, but, in all the important things, no different. Red ears, pointed nose. I stroked them tenderly. How fine they were this morning!

I got up. It was easy. I just asked myself to do it. I sat down. I got up. I went to the window. I looked out. It was raining hard. Water, essential to life. How apt! Rain soaking the back lawn. Everything growing. Trees swaying in the breeze. Leaves, a few birds.

Wonderful sights!

I looked on them as I'd never looked before. Humbled, thankful.

I had no fear of what was to come. The Minister was

waiting, but I was alive. I *wanted* to see him. Now I loved him, and soon he would love me.

Love, family, trees, rain. The simple things. No more jazz, or pin-up pictures. No more seditious books, single-bar Bellings. No more dope. Certainly no more dope!

I went to the bathroom and ran a bath. Then I soaked myself, soaping away the past in a kind of baptism. It was truly the end of an era. I felt clean, refreshed. Maybe I'd take up golf again. It was too late to be a new Arnold Palmer, too late for many things, but a great chunk of my life was ahead of me and there was still time to make good at something now that the Bomber was being flushed away.

I dressed in a clean shirt and a fresh V-neck sweater. I dug out a pair of trousers, flannel ones that itched my legs. Then I combed my hair, parting it on the left, flattening it down with water. A new me, just like everyone else. Alive, normal.

I went downstairs to meet my makers, remorse, gratitude and a new imperative for reparation flooding my breast as with each step my feet met the worn stair carpet. The Minister and Mary were both in the living room. Mary was dabbing at her eyes with a handkerchief. I could tell she hadn't slept. I wanted to reach out and clutch her for her dishevelled state was suddenly an all too eloquent testimony to the countless nights without sleep she'd endured on my behalf. The blinds were drawn. I thought about going over to them, opening them up, letting the light flood in in one glorious symbolic gesture that would relieve everybody at once. But I just stood at the door, contrite, clasping my hands in front of me, with my head slightly bowed. There was silence except for Mary's occasional sniffling. The Minister peered at me over his specs. He looked long and hard as though trying to penetrate the depths of my very soul. Eventually he spoke. His voice was quiet, deliberate, evincing a dogged attempt at control.

'Well, my lad,' he said. 'What have you got to say for yourself?'

I knew what he expected. A smart-alecky comeback, a rebellious tone, dumb insolence, eyes looking past him into the garden. I saw him brace himself against his own furious response.

I looked at him unflinchingly. Then in a tone of bell-like sincerity answered his question.

'I'm sorry,' I said simply. 'I'm sorry.'

I tried to invest the words with all that I now regretted in my past, and all I hoped for in the future – in fact, with proof of their meaning. But they were strange words, new to me. I felt clumsy saying them, just as you do when you speak the first words of a new language. Still, something of my intent must have got into them for the Minister, having pivoted forwards on his elbows ready to leap at me the moment I opened my mouth, stopped as the words registered, and his verbal response to the insult he'd expected to hear faltered on his lips in a smothered, dumbfounded grunt.

'I'm sorry,' I said again. 'For everything.'

I raised my arms in an all-embracing sign, then dropped them helplessly. I could say nothing more for it was all too poignantly dramatic. The Minister swung there for a moment on his elbows, then he pulled himself to his feet and came over to me. He stood close, gazing at me. I raised my head. We looked at each other, father and son, man to man. Then he reached out his hand, took mine, and shook it. A great tear rolled down my cheek. Suddenly the house was full of joy, forgiveness, light. Mary sobbed happily. For so long she had waited and prayed! Now the moment had come. He that had been lost was found. He that had been

163

blind could see.

I sat down next to her on the sofa. From time to time she patted my knee, the expression on her face a mixture of pride and gratitude. The three of us beamed at one another, almost painfully shy in our new community. Then Mary went off to make tea.

'The rules,' the Minister began. 'Life can be good if you don't flout the rules.'

I nodded earnestly. I knew what he meant for I had just returned from the brink.

'Careers, marriage, getting on,' he continued. 'These aren't things to deny. They've always been there. They distinguish us from animals. They make for progress. Think of the wheel, the light bulb, the aeroplane. Nothing comes out of nothing!'

How wise he was! How clear! If only I'd listened to him before! But this was the dawn of a new era, with no place for regrets. I thought only of the wheel, the light bulb and the aeroplane. Progress. The real world. Now I was a part of it. I felt five years, no, ten years older than the day before. Mature, responsible, ready to do my bit.

Mary came back with the tea. She poured. We all sipped. There were no recriminations, no mention of jam or Williams. The change was obvious. A new spirit of co-operation and mutual regard prevailed.

'Let's get down to basics,' the Minister said. 'What are you good at?'

'English,' I said.

I caught myself anticipating his gutteral 'Ach!' of contempt, but it didn't come. He got up, found paper and pens, then we started a list. It was a slow halting start with few interesting alternatives. After an hour we had only two: management training, and librarianship. Neither sat well, but the Minister could hardly contain his enthusiasm.

'Don't worry,' he told me. 'One minute you're listening to jazz, the next you're settling down to a responsible job. It happens to all of us, I thought you were an exception. But no, the world turns. All rivers still run to the sea.'

With that homily the issue seemed settled. The Minister laid aside paper and pen, then looked at me. I think I was supposed to state my preference. Suddenly the real world didn't look quite such an attractive proposition. There had to be another alternative. My eyes shifted around the room as I tried to avoid his. Vaguely, I took in the furniture. I wasn't about to betray the new mood, or welch on unspoken agreements, but I didn't want to spend my life managing the floor of a shop or grappling with the complexities of the Dewey decimal system. With mounting distress my eyes roved over the lamp standards, the carpets, the old TV, the radiogram. Then they fell on a crumpled newspaper resting on the arm of an empty chair in the room. All at once I broke into a grin. Eureka! Man bites dog! I sat bolt upright, snapping my fingers.

'Newspapers!' I exclaimed. 'Journalism. I think I'd like to be a reporter.'

Oh, happy day! In one fell swoop I'd returned to the bosom of my family and discovered what I wanted to do with my life. It was just as the Minister said. When you stopped flouting the rules it all came to you. I was living proof of the matter – a man with a mission. I could just see myself, a member of that courageous fraternity of men travelling the world, on call at a moment's notice, braving jungles, war zones, and criminal underworlds to uphold the principles of democracy and the freedom of the Press.

I sat back, waiting for the Minister's reponse. Slowly he nodded.

'Yes,' he said. 'You might just do it. Of course, it'll mean hard work. You'd have to start at the bottom. It won't be easy. Plenty of disappointments.'

But I barely heard him, so flushed and keen was I with my timely and fitting selection.

I spent my eighteenth birthday equipping myself for the brave new world of adulthood. I went into town with Mary (she was 'mother' now, and the Minister was 'father'), and bought clothes, sensible clothes that befitted my new seriousness and sense of responsibility. Sturdy, cuffless trousers in dark green corduroy, of a discreet width – not too tight, not too baggy. Stout shoes to do the rounds in. A brown woollen jacket with a single vent at the back. Even a couple of ties. These clothes were the family's gift to me, twenty pounds' worth bought from men's outfitters I would have scorned as unbeat only a week before. If I was to mingle at large in the world, ceaselessly probing to unearth scandal and crime, then I couldn't afford to cause any offence, I'd have to be all things to all men.

At home I tried everything on. I creaked a little in the shoes, and the tie felt like a noose, but I certainly looked the part. Upstairs in my room I clipped six or seven pencils and pens into the outside top pocket of the jacket, a nice touch to complete the impression. Then I went down.

'Voilà,' I said in impeccable French.

My mother gaped, pleased as Punch with my purchases.

'You look very smart, dear,' was all she could manage.

The ultimate seal of approval came when the Minister took me down to the local. He never went into a pub, but there we sat in The Crown sipping halves of shandy together, toasting my glittering future. The Crown wasn't the Crucible by any manner or means, but I felt splendid just sitting there, smiling to myself over the quirky turn of events. Shandy, new shoes, pencils in my top pocket – these, after all, were the wonderful things which had beckoned.

I pulled out my present to myself, a briar pipe, one of two I'd picked up the same afternoon. For some reason I thought all reporters smoked pipes. I filled a bowl, and lit up. I felt substantial, solid. I leant back in my seat, puffing. It didn't taste good and my tongue furred over, but I still persevered. Soon my new clothes would smell of shag. I was engulfed in smoke, great clouds rising from me.

That evening I wrote to the local newspaper requesting an opening. My letter was long, laid out according to the rules which I'd learned at prep school. My address at the top right. Dear Sir. Yours faithfully. In between I tried to demonstrate my enthusiasm and aptitude for the profession. I'd take anything to begin with, I wrote. I'd start at the bottom, learning the craft from the ground up. I said I'd work hard. I knew it wouldn't be easy, but I was sure I'd make good for I'd always excelled at English.

Confidently, I awaited a reply. Meanwhile, I bought spiral-topped notebooks and practised smoking my pipes. One day I cleaned out my room. I boxed up the records and books. I dismantled the Belling. Finally I came to my scrapbook. It was hard to dump that, but after one last sneaky flick through I eventually managed it. Poor Brigitte, consigned to the bin of the past along with all the other devices of boyhood.

An answer came back from the *Echo* three or four days later. By then I'd filled a couple of books with scribbled notes for various scoops, and I was practically pipe smoker of the year so I wasn't surprised I was up for the post of Assistant Editor at one of the newspaper's district offices. As far as I was concerned it was merely the first of many predetermined arrangements by which I'd follow my vocation. Even so, I was pleased. I'd barely begun yet here I was an assistant editor already. The interview would be a formality. Against 'scoop' Selby, veteran reporter of the widespread abuse of exotic substances, no other candidate would stand a chance.

The following week the old fellow took me to meet the board. I was brimful of confidence, dressed in my new clothes, smelling of coarse-cut tobacco. I sat by the door of the interview room with one other person, a pimply youth with dandruff on the shoulders of a non-descript suit. He was called in before me. He came out fifteen minutes later, white-faced, shaking his head despondently. Then it was my turn. Inside were two men, both smoking pipes! One of them, the proprietor and overall editor, was huge, a veritable Citizen Kane. The other was small and bald with a dome-shaped head, lacklustre eyes, and drab beige-coloured clothes. This was the editor of the district office. It was he who asked the obvious question, the old chestnut about essential qualities.

'Initiative, energy, and a flair for English,' I barked back instantly.

Both men were impressed. They looked at each other, nodding. Then the small one asked: 'When can you start?'

'The sooner the better,' I said.

For the second time in two months I was welcomed aboard. My new boss explained the conditions of my contract (with a letter to follow), gave me details of where to go, and how to get there. Then, after congratulations, I left.

The old fellow was tickled pink by the news. On our way home we had two more shandies to celebrate.

168

18

The first day of a life's work, a milestone on a journey, a day to treasure, one to look back upon from the dizzy pinnacle of a brilliant career and recall with satisfaction in the years to come – yes, the seeds of my achievements were all sown then!

I got up, I washed and dressed. I clipped in my pens. I went down to breakfast. It was a man's breakfast, bacon, eggs and tomatoes, just like the Minister's. There was that quietness there often is amongst men at the start of a new working week. We read the papers, drank tea, hardly spoke. Mary was more nervous than I was.

'You're not nervous, are you, dear?'

The words of a mother. I looked up from my tea, a look that said: 'Nervous? Why, no, for I'm a reporter with nerves of steel. Where would I be, a nervous reporter in the world of men?'

169

Briefly I glanced at the Minister. His amused eyes glittered back at mine. What did women know of our men's business? I smiled indulgently at her.

'No,' I replied. 'Just eager.'

She busied herself by making more tea, a happy woman unravelled from the cares of the past. Today she would go out, holding her head high, aglow with the achievements of a mother whose duties have been successfully dispatched.

'How's that Ned of your's coming along, Mrs Selby?'

No hesitancy now. A broad smile, confident voice:

'Very well indeed, thank you. Working hard, you know. On the *Echo*. He's barely begun but already he's an assistant editor.'

An adequate title for the time being. But it wouldn't suit me for long. As I sat back smoking my first bowl of the day I sketched out my meteoric rise: district editor within six months, a triumphant spell on the crime desk in town, finally the call from Fleet Street.

'Well, Ned, are you ready?' the Minister asked.

Ready? I was chomping at the bit. I grabbed one of my notebooks and waited at the door. Mary kissed us both, seeing her men off in the time-honoured fashion of mothers and wives. I fancied the phrase 'Don't do anything silly' trembled on her lips when she waved one last time, but she held it back, reassured once again by the vision of a new me in dark green cords and a sensible jacket.

It was a ten-minute trip to the railway station. The Minister and I still didn't speak, although the car seemed clamorous with our memories, numberless recollections of a misspent youth which was now a harmless, amusing thing, just a series of tangled incidents at last conceded to the past.

I bought my ticket, a season ticket as a token of my new sense of order and permanence. It was ennobling, this badge

170

of maturity in its crisp plastic folder, and I slipped it, three months' worth of journeys to and from work, behind my pens. The Minister stood waiting, then we walked onto the platform, he to go his way to London, me to go mine out into the heart of the Fens. We parted simply.

'Good luck,' he said with a smile.

'Thank you, father,' I answered, the calmness of my voice belying the sudden flurry of feelings which jostled for pride of place in my breast – gratitude, affection, the now undeniable bond of blood.

'Thank you,' I said again.

Then I turned and walked to my train. I chose an empty carriage since I wanted to gather my thoughts and engage an alertness for the great enterprise to come. I placed my notebook on my knees and flicked back the cover. 'Monday,' I wrote. Then I added: 'Day One'. After another pause I put: 'D-Day'. I was going great guns, an uninterrupted flow of critical information.

A whistle blew, the train shuddered, suddenly I was on my way. I made a note of the time. Seven forty-five. Weather fair, visibility good, a low damp mist enveloping the Fens. What on earth was out there, I wondered. It was an uninviting marshy region, no doubt inhabited by strange, retarded folk still locked in all the old ways. A place where cousins still married cousins, and farm workers still did unspeakable things to ewes. A dangerous, mysterious place, none better suited for the attentions of a reporter of my mettle and calibre.

For twenty-five minutes the train rattled through this bleak landscape, then it slowed into a small station. It wasn't much – trim gardens, Victorian ticket office, a couple of platforms – no different from a thousand others, but this was my station.

I opened the door and climbed down. For a moment I stood still, taking everything in. Then I walked to the gate, showing my ticket to the collector.

'My name's Selby,' I told him. 'Ned Selby. I just thought I'd make your acquaintance. I'm a reporter, you see. I need a contact here at the station. For information. Robberies, crashes, people throwing themselves from the trains. Let me know if anything happens. Selby's the name. The new man at the *Echo*.'

The collector gawped open-mouthed, then he took one step back into his cubicle. Perhaps I'd rushed him. These relationships took time to establish, especially out here where people were naturally suspicious of strangers.

Briskly, I walked into town. In fact it was hardly more than a village. The buildings and people I passed seemed to exude a fastidiously genteel air, but it didn't fool me for a minute. Small though it was, the whole place reeked. There was the Town Hall, a hotbed of corruption! There, the church with the profligate vicar! There, the school on the verge of collapse! In a week or two I'd begin my campaigns, clean-up campaigns with words and pictures. Blankets covering faces, angry crowds, many dead. Stories by Ned Selby, the new man at the *Echo*.

I strode on in the purposeful gait of a reporter, my mind buzzing with these projects. Then abruptly I stopped. Emblazoned on the front of a building was the newspaper's logo in bold red letters. I saw it at once, my eyes drawn to it as if to a beacon of flames. I murmured the name. It was a good name for a paper, signifying much more to me than a mere reflection of what already was. My echo would ring with the truth, and its infinite reverberations would spread out to touch all sections of this troubled community.

I crossed to the High Street and approached the building

172

with a kind of pride, the many responsibilities of my vocation swarming to me.

Twenty minutes later I was ensconced in my new office. It was a big room, befitting my sense of importance. On the desk was a white phone, an old Olivetti Imperial, a *Pitman's Shorthand*, and a new ream of paper. Already I'd been hard at it, calling the police.

'Selby at the *Echo* here,' I'd boomed out confidently. 'Anything to report?'

There'd been nothing. Still, you couldn't help but admire the way I'd asked. Now I sucked on my pipe and examined the Imperial. It was black, a delicate machine, the most important tool of my trade. Gingerly, I released the carriage. It rang beautifully. I fed in a clean sheet of paper, squaring it carefully. Then I cracked my knuckles, flexed my fingers, and let rip. I typed the letter X. I typed it again, several more times. I filled up two lines with Xs, concentrating on accuracy rather than speed. Finally, using two fingers, I banged out my name and address, crisp, clean print whipped off in a couple of minutes. I was amazed by my aptitude. My fingers stabbed at the keys, four of them now, in fluent rhythmic bursts punctuated by the sound of the bell. For over an hour I practised, then Firstin, the district editor, stepped into my office.

'I've got something for you,' he announced grandly.

Instantly, I stopped clattering. I felt a sudden sharp thrill of anticipation. My first story! Soon I'd be down at the Town Hall, my skilful questions eliciting incriminating information from the mouths of the unwary.

'Yes,' he went on keenly. 'In at the deep end. I can see

173

you're raring to go.'

I acknowledged his confidence with a casual grin, then waited for the assignment.

'Run over to the Women's Institute,' he said. 'They're having a sale.'

'Ah,' I exclaimed. 'Of stolen goods.'

Firstin looked at me queerly, as though he hadn't quite grasped what I'd meant.

'Jumble,' he said simply.

Now it was my turn to frown.

'You mean old clothes, broken appliances?'

'Yes,' he said, 'that sort of stuff.'

I studied his face, sensing I was being put to some kind of test. It was a bland face, ordinary. But I knew this was a mask, a convenient disguise for a vigorous investigative spirit.

'What's the angle?' I asked quickly.

Then before he could speak, it burst in on me.

'Of course!' I shouted, pounding the desk with my hand. 'The old girls are fiddling the receipts, cheating the charity.'

I jumped to my feet, instinctively checking my pockets for pencils and notebook.

'Don't worry,' I said. 'Initiative! Energy! A flair for English. I'll leave no stone unturned. It'll be a scoop, feathers in both our caps.'

Firstin's face filled with consternation. He blocked the doorway as I went hurtling towards it. Aghast, he stretched out his arms.

'Good God!' he cried, in a flustered, protesting voice. 'These are the wives of local luminaries . . .'

'Looting wives of local luminaries,' I barked. 'What a headline! "Selby rumbles the jumbles".'

'I'm talking about vicars, school teachers,' Firstin

objected urgently. 'Pillars of the community.'

'Yes,' I said. 'But we're reporters, members of that happy breed of men as yet untamed by immoderate reverence for officialdom. Strip away the comfortable veneer of rural respectability and what do you find: greed, hypocrisy, Peyton Place.'

Firstin gazed at me. I saw his face gradually break into a grin, then all of a sudden he was laughing, peals of laughter rolling from him.

'Oh that's good,' he gasped, pausing for breath. 'Very good. What did you say? Angle? Scoop? Had me completely fooled for a minute.'

Then he was off again, slapping his thighs, hooting with uncontrollable mirth.

I stood there listening to him laugh, overwhelmed by the scale of my folly. Finally, he recovered. I left just as soon as I could, faking a grin for his benefit.

The sale was as dull as I now knew it would be: stout women in tweeds doing their bit for the church fund. Afterwards I took a long sobering walk through the town. Now that too was unutterably prosaic. Resigned, I sat on a bench. I pulled out my pipe for a smoke before going back to the office. Instead, quite suddenly I snapped it, tossing the pieces aside. Then I got up.

I spent the rest of the day typing the news. A simple story: five lines, who, what, why, where and when.

It happens to everybody: one minute you're listening to jazz, the next you're settling down to a responsible job.

19

Now I was one of the crowd. It was a routine existence, with nothing untoward, and no surprises. Each working day passed exactly like the next. I got up at the same time, ate the same breakfast, caught the same train, found the same carriage, sat in the same seat. I arrived at the office at the usual time, opened up in the usual way. I phoned the police, I phoned the fire station. Each morning I vaguely hoped for murder and arson. Each morning I was vaguely disappointed. The *Echo*, at least our page on it, had other concerns anyway: births, marriages and deaths. Mostly, that's what life was, Firstin said.

Once in a long while there'd be a retirement presentation: some old codger – Firstin fifteen years on, or me forty-five – receiving a salver in EPNS for a lifetime's loyal and devoted service. Tears would gush. Tales would be told. Half a dozen lines of clipped information would appear in the following

Friday's edition. One man's life. Extra! Extra! Read all about it!

When I wasn't out and about, I'd be found in my office practising shorthand for all I was worth so that when the big one came – that exclusive scoop – I'd be ready. It never did, though there were times when I felt a glimmer of the excited enthusiasm which had accompanied my first walk from the station. One night I covered the Rotary Club's Amateur Players' performance of *Lady Windermere's Fan*, an occasion made unforgettable by missed cues, early entrances and collapsing scenery. My pencil flew across spiral-bound pages, immaculate shorthand panning all and sundry in brisk, terse sentences. Inevitably, the final review came back, along with Firstin's memo: praise everyone, upset nobody, remember the advertising.

There were compensations, of course. Eighteen pounds a week, most of which I banked. Quiet evenings at home. My place on the sofa. The Minister and I suddenly finding something in common: an obsession with bad management, bosses we both disliked and whose jobs we knew we could do better. Those nights I'd suck on my remaining pipe and we'd grumble and debate together whilst Mary sewed or brought tea and biscuits at frequent intervals.

Sometimes I thought about the past but when I did so I was aware that I was investing those times with all the phoney brightness of youth, that brief transit of illusory delights which occurs before the imperatives of adult life take over.

I'd grown up; everybody said I had.

One day I noticed I was losing my hair. At first it was a shock, the appearance of a scar below my hair-line which until then had been hidden above, but even that didn't faze me for long. In a year I'd look distinguished, with a bright,

177

shiny pate just like the Minister's.

Tentatively, I took up golf again. I'd lost some of the old skill, but I quickly became a good weekend player, able to hold my own with all the others.

Two months passed. Three. All in all it was a comfortable life. Occasionally, I was bored with the repetition, but then who wasn't? Life, as the Minister often said, was a matter of light breezes rather than fierce winds and, in his estimation, all the better for it. What I needed for complete peace of mind, he suggested, was a girl. Someone solid. Someone reliable. Someone like Agate.

To begin with I was simply amused by the idea. I never would have believed I'd hear the Minister encourage such a liaison. Yet in a way I was flattered, too, for it was an index of his confidence in my newfound sense and stability. Once upon a time he'd determined she was far too good for me.

At any rate, I dismissed his suggestion, but in the weeks that followed it gradually came back to haunt me. Light breezes were all very well, but those in my life were beginning to feel merely timid. Companionship, sex, would no doubt liven them up, providing a welcome buffer against those moments of tedium which I noticed were growing more and more frequent with the passing weeks.

Agate. She was a nice girl, kind and considerate. In spite of myself I started to remember details. Musical evenings, Italian meals, starched uniforms. At odd moments of the day I'd visualise her face. Late at night, after TV closedown, I'd find myself listening for the click of the front bedroom light, and when I heard that old signal I'd instantly fall into fevered reverie – her thighs, her fine big arse. Yes, perhaps we *could* get together again. There was certainly no harm in trying.

Many times I hovered over the phone, hesitant, nervous,

maybe even a little confused. But finally I lifted the receiver.

What happened next came as a bolt from the blue. Suddenly I broke into a violent cold sweat. I threw the phone down at the fourth ring. I rushed upstairs to the bathroom, knelt over the pan and puked and puked and puked.

When that was done I staggered to my room and flopped down. I knew I'd had some sort of fit, a real one this time, though at precisely the moment it happened, when I was clutching the phone, waiting, I did have a fleeting sensation that I was locked in a cupboard. Trapped some place, anyway.

Now, on the bed, after emptying myself, I felt – well, unimpeded. I felt wretched, of course, that is, weak, and still a little nauseous, but I also felt oddly composed as if in that mammoth puke something had come together as well as having come up and out. It wasn't just Agate on whom I'd thrown down the phone. It was on me. Or at least on some unconsummated view of myself which I'd suddenly caught sight of. My God, there I'd been, entwined on the sofa with Agate, forever waiting on the click of the light, forever waiting for my life to begin.

I was depressed for days after the incident, in vain trying to avoid the inevitable. The Minister and Mary sensed something was up for I spent evenings alone in my room. Mostly I just thought or read, but one night I unboxed my records. For I while I just flicked through them, as though flicking through old photographs, each one fixed in time, but eventually I couldn't help myself. Errol's piano got right down inside me the way it always had done, connecting me once again to a strain of feelings I'd sought to deny. It wasn't the adolescent dreamer I'd regained – I knew I could no longer exist on dreams. It was simply a notion that there was something more to life than district offices and sofas, a faith, if you like, in the power of exuberance.

After that my departure was merely a matter of timing. For a while I hoped I might be able to explain so I lingered at home restless, distracted, waiting for the opportunity. It didn't come nor, as I soon realised, would it ever come. I slipped out one Saturday morning, leaving a note. Paris, it wasn't my spiritual home. But it was as good a place as any in which to start coming to grips with myself. Maybe I wouldn't amount to much. Maybe I'd eventually wind up back on the sofa. But if I did at least I'd know I'd been out there, checking a few of the alternatives first.